'I don't intend

'A case of "Alw[...]
bride"!' vowed Cl[...]

'Just as well,' muttered Alain under his breath.

Suddenly, amid the laughing, milling crowd, it was as if they were alone.

'Why do you say that?' she challenged, hating herself for rising to the bait, but unable to resist.

'Because I can't imagine you ever being content with one man,' was the cruel reply.

Dear Reader

Friends can help make Christmas an extra-special time for us all . . . so you can be sure that your friends at Mills & Boon have chosen these four books especially to enhance your enjoyment of the festive season. As all good things should be, our novels are available all year round, so why not make it your resolution to enjoy a little romance every month of the coming year?

Happy Christmas,

The Editor

Angela Devine grew up in Tasmania surrounded by forests, mountains and wild seas, so she dislikes big cities. Before taking up writing, she worked as a teacher, librarian and university lecturer. As a young mother and Ph.D. student, she read romantic fiction for fun and later decided it would be even more fun to write it. She is married with four children, loves chocolate and Twinings teas and hates ironing. Her current hobbies are gardening, bushwalking, travelling and classical music.

Recent titles by the same author:

SEED OF THE FIRE LILY

TAHITIAN WEDDING

BY
ANGELA DEVINE

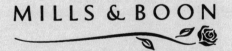

MILLS & BOON LIMITED
ETON HOUSE, 18-24 PARADISE ROAD
RICHMOND, SURREY TW9 1SR

To my mother,
the world's champion babysitter.

First published in Great Britain in 1993
by Mills & Boon Limited

© Angela Devine 1993

Australian copyright 1993
Philippine copyright 1993
This edition 1993

ISBN 0 263 78043 0

Set in Times Roman 10 on 11 pt
94-9311-58080 C

Made and printed in Great Britain

CHAPTER ONE

THE plane bucked friskily. Bells chimed a warning and down the long cavern of the interior the 'fasten seat-belts' signs lit up. With the ease of long practice Claire came out of her doze, flung back the lightweight blue blanket and sat up straight. As she cinched the seatbelt firmly round her waist, she gazed out of the window with a troubled frown. It was not the motion of the plane that worried her. Minor air turbulence was something she could deal with, but the turbulence in her feelings was another matter entirely.

Going home to Tahiti for the first time in years thrilled her to the core and she was genuinely excited at the prospect of her sister Marie Rose's wedding. Yet she could not shake off the feeling of dread that weighed on her more heavily with each passing minute. And there could be no doubt about the cause of her uneasiness. What disturbed her was the fear that she would meet the man who had driven her away from home in the first place. The one man in the world capable of turning elegant, sophisticated Claire Beaumont to a quivering mass of jelly. A man who seemed perfectly charming on the surface, but was capable of being ruthless, forceful and terrifyingly stern. Alain Charpentier. Alain, whom she had idolised for a few brief months. Until something happened which had ruined his good opinion of her forever.

Restlessly Claire pushed up the sliding shutter which covered the window and pressed her face to the glass. Outside it was dark except for the light of a single star which winked out like the flash of a solitaire diamond.

Far ahead the blackness was still impenetrable with no sign of the South Pacific Islands which were her destination. Yet Claire's watch showed almost four-fifteen a.m. It could not be long before the Air New Zealand plane touched down in Papeete and she had to face the ordeal ahead. Her stomach churned with nerves at the thought, but she gritted her teeth, picked up her toiletries bag and made her way down the aisle to freshen up. Five minutes later she was back in her seat with her long, dark brown hair combed into a smooth bun, discreet eyeshadow accentuating her lustrous brown eyes and a touch of blusher on her high cheekbones. And, as always, her clothes were impeccable. A lightweight jade-green dress with white trim around the neckline and short sleeves, which she had bought in Marseilles the previous summer. And white basket-weave sandals and matching shoulder-bag from Florence. There were some advantages to constant international travel, thought Claire wryly, although not as many as most people thought.

'Say, don't I know you from somewhere, honey?' exclaimed a startled American voice.

The woman paused in the aisle, clutching the back of a seat to steady herself as another flurry of air turbulence hit the plane.

'You're the spitting image of the girl reporter in that TV show *Towards the Future*. What's her name now? Claire Bowman?'

Claire grinned and held out her hand.

'Claire Beaumont,' she agreed.

'Oh, wow, that's really something,' said the woman. 'I've never met anybody famous before. My name's Sarah Howard and that's my husband Norman. Norm, come on over here. Just wait until you hear who this is.'

Claire smiled until her cheeks ached, while Sarah and Norman questioned her excitedly about life as an international reporter. She was touched by their warmth but it was a relief when the captain announced the plane's impending descent. As she sank back into her seat, a deep pang of longing flooded through Claire. All the fame in the world could never compensate her for the things which were still missing from her life. Love. A real home. A family.

The lights of Papeete began to show white and sulphur-yellow beneath the plane's wing, and Claire leaned forward eagerly. It was six years since she had been home and a fever of impatience gripped her now as the plane's engines screamed and the tarmac came hurtling towards her. There was a faint bump, then the plane taxied to a halt about fifty metres from the terminal. Stepping out on to the ramp, she took a deep breath of the warm, moist tropical air. High on the bank surrounding the airport, coconut palms waved their feathery tops and the cloying scent of frangipani drifted from unseen gardens. Ahead of her lay the terminal building, constructed in the Polynesian style with swooping gables and thatched roofs. And, somewhere inside, her sister Marie Rose should be waiting to meet her. Marie Rose, who would no doubt be bubbling with news about her forthcoming wedding and Claire's role as bridesmaid at it. The thought of seeing her sister again filled Claire with excitement but also a faint, uneasy misgiving. She couldn't help dreading that Marie Rose would probe into her secret reason for staying away so long.

Yet it was not Marie Rose who came forward to greet her as she emerged from Customs. It was somebody else. And, as Claire saw that lean, dark, unsmiling figure striding across the polished vinyl floor, her heart skipped a beat.

She had not seen him for six years, but every nerve in her body was clamouring recognition. He had not changed much. His frame was as lithe and muscular as ever and his face was still satanically handsome. She had always realised that he was good looking. Yet, staring

at that springy, dark hair, those intense cornflower-blue
eyes and that finely chiselled nose, Claire was stunned
anew at the vibrant animal magnetism that Alain
Charpentier exuded. In fact, if it had not been for a
sardonic twist to the well shaped mouth and a stormy
look in his blue eyes, he would have been downright irresistible. He wore a navy and white short-sleeved shirt
that had the indefinable stamp of quality, tailored navy
shorts and rope-soled espadrilles. Obviously his habit of
being casually well dressed had not changed since the
last time they had met. Yet there was something else that
had not changed in Alain Charpentier: his hostility towards Claire.

As he came to a halt in front of her there was no hint
of a smile on his lips. Nevertheless, his manners were as
impeccable as ever. Placing a lei of fragrant frangipani
blossoms over her head, he kissed her formally on both
cheeks. Claire was shaken by that contact. Alain's
powerful fingers were gripping her shoulders and she
caught the whiff of an expensive cologne as his warm
cheek touched hers. An odd, fluttering sensation
quivered deep inside her. Perhaps, after all this time, we
can finally be friends, she thought. Yet there was nothing
friendly in Alain's manner as he released her. His eyes
wandered down over her body with a brooding hostility
that stung her unbearably.

'So. After six years you finally honour us with your
presence,' he drawled insultingly.

Claire's brown eyes blazed.

'Did you think you could keep me out of Tahiti
forever?' she demanded. 'I'm not a gullible nineteen-
year-old any more, you know. So if you're planning to
order me out of the country again, don't bother!'

Alain's bottom lip curled.

'I see,' he said with heavy irony. 'So I am the reason
that you haven't come home for six years, am I? I'm

flattered. I didn't know my desires meant so much to you.'

'They don't!' retorted Claire in a furious whisper, conscious of the interested glances of other travellers. 'But if I remember correctly, last time we met you told me you never wanted to see me in Tahiti again.'

'You do remember correctly,' agreed Alain. 'Just as I do, Claire. Not one word or one action of yours has been forgiven or forgotten. But for the sake of Marie Rose I am prepared to be polite to you during this visit.'

Claire seethed at the antagonism in his tone, but his words were a nagging reminder of something else. Gazing impatiently round the building, she looked in vain for her sister.

'Where is Marie Rose?' she demanded. 'She promised to come and meet me.'

'Unfortunately she was not able to do it,' replied Alain. 'She asked me to come in her place.'

'What's wrong?' asked Claire in alarm. 'She's not ill, is she?'

Alain dismissed that with a shrug.

'Marie Rose? No! But for your father, it's a different matter. His heart has been giving him trouble for the last two years, although perhaps you didn't know or care about that.'

'I knew,' replied Claire shortly. 'And I cared.'

'But not enough to come home and visit him?' challenged Alain.

Claire bit her lip, but remained silent. Alain's barbed comments filled her with guilt. Knowing Alain, that was probably just what he intended. After all, he had never hidden his opinion that Claire was heartless and totally indifferent to other people's feelings. In fact, her father's illness troubled Claire deeply, but pride would not allow her to tell Alain the truth—that she had repeatedly tried and failed to persuade Roland Beaumont to visit a Sydney heart specialist at her expense. As for visiting her family, her conscience was quite clear on that score. Fear of meeting Alain had always kept her away from Tahiti, but she had paid several times for her parents and sister to join her in Sydney. Yet why should she have to justify herself to Alain by explaining all this?

'Well,' said Alain with a lift of his eyebrow, 'there will be plenty of time to catch up on the rest of the news in my car. For now, I think we should go and collect your luggage. After that, I will take you to meet Marie Rose and your parents, just as she asked.'

Claire stared at him in perplexity.

'But why should Marie Rose ask you to do all that?' she demanded. 'You hardly knew her.'

'Six years ago, no,' agreed Alain. 'But a lot can happen in six years. Didn't Marie Rose tell you that her fiancé Paul Halévy is my cousin and the manager of my new hotel on Moorea?'

Claire took a step back.

'No, she didn't!' she replied in a startled voice.

Alain smiled sardonically.

'Then, in that case, she probably did not tell you either that I am to be best man at her wedding. Am I right?'

This time Claire stared at him in horror.

'Best man?' she croaked. 'That's impossible! Ridiculous!'

'Believe me,' Alain assured her, 'the thought of being constantly thrown into your company for the next week is just as unwelcome to me as it must be to you. But for the sake of Marie Rose and Paul, we must both put a good face on it. Now come and we'll collect your luggage. You must be tired after your long trip.'

Claire's thoughts whirled as Alain whisked her through the building. For one insane moment she was tempted to flee back to the plane she had just left, but Alain was handling her arrival as efficiently as he had once or- ganised her departure. With the ease of a man accus- tomed to prompt service, he soon had her outside the

airport and comfortably settled in the luxurious front
seat of his gleaming Citroën car.

'You travel light,' he observed. 'Only one small
suitcase on wheels. As if you were always ready for a
fast getaway.'

Claire shrugged.

'That's truer than you know,' she agreed. 'I've been
on the move so much in the last six years that I've re-
duced it to a fine art. I never own more than I can carry.'

'That must be difficult,' observed Alain.

'Not really. It's very simple. All you have to do is
decide never to get attached to things.'

'Or people?' Alain challenged.

'Or people!' retorted Claire with a defiant toss of her
head.

Settling back into her seat, she folded her arms and
stared resentfully ahead of her into the darkness. He was
determined to goad her, she thought fiercely, but she
wasn't going to be drawn. Alain Charpentier had made
a blistering attack on her morals and her character once
in her life, but she certainly wasn't going to give him a
second opportunity.

'You've done very well since you left Tahiti,' he said
in milder voice. 'You should be very proud of yourself.'

'Thank you,' replied Claire coolly.

'Of course it's not the sort of lifestyle that would suit
everybody,' continued Alain. 'I've always admired your
poise in front of the cameras and your ability to adapt
to new countries, but I should imagine that sort of jet-
setting must be very exhausting. It's a good thing you've
never wanted a settled home or any serious attachments,
isn't it?'

'Yes, isn't it?' retorted Claire with an edge to her voice.

She stared out the window again and an ache like a
physical pain filled her entire body. Her throat tightened
as she remembered how often she had cried herself to
sleep in her first bewildering months in Sydney. How

many times had she felt a sharp, nostalgic longing for Tahiti, simply because of some trivial reminder that had sent her thoughts winging back to her home? The scent of warm croissants outside a bakery, the sight of scarlet bougainvillaea spilling over a balcony, the feathery crown of a coconut palm waving against a blue sky had all been enough to reduce her to tears. But worst of all had been the pain of missing her family. Her easygoing father Roland, with his rumbling laugh and his home handyman projects that never quite worked, her mother Eve, who sometimes surfaced from her painting long enough to cook wonderful French meals, not to mention her numerous aunts and uncles and cousins. And, of course, warm-hearted Marie Rose, whose only fault was her well-meaning desire to get Claire married off as soon as possible. How dared Alain assume that Claire's home meant nothing to her or that she didn't want deep attachments to anyone? Unconsciously she leaned forward urgently, as if she could make the car go faster.

'We should be there just as the sun rises,' she said. 'I do hope we can reach Point Cupid before it comes up! I always used to love watching it from that bare hillside overlooking the bay.'

'Did you?' asked Alain. 'Well, I'll be glad to stop and let you see it, but I should warn you that the hillside is no longer bare. I've built a hotel there.'

'You've what?' cried Claire in horror. 'Oh, how could you, Alain? How could you possibly ruin that beautiful headland by building some ghastly eyesore of a hotel there? Don't you have any sensitivity at all?'

To her astonishment the car suddenly veered sharply off the road and came to halt. The glow from one of the sulphur-yellow street-lights filled the vehicle's interior, turning Alain's face to a bronze mask as he turned off the ignition. Then he seized her wrist, and glared down at her.

'No,' he said through his teeth. 'I am like you in that respect, Claire. I have no sensitivity whatsoever and you would do well to remember it. And like you, I care only about one thing—the satisfaction of my own desires. All the same, I flatter myself that I do have good taste. So why don't you wait until you've seen the hotel before you condemn it as being ghastly? It seems to me that you're entirely too willing to make judgements about situations without being in full possession of the facts!'

'Really?' retorted Claire. 'I always thought that was your speciality!'

'You go too far!' grated Alain.

His glittering blue eyes narrowed as he stared down at her and she caught her breath in a swift, convulsive gulp. The movement made her breasts strain against the low-cut neckline of her dress and she was conscious of the swift, instinctive flare of desire in Alain's glance. Against her will Claire felt an answering surge of excitement as his eyes rose to scan her face. The silence lengthened and Claire was conscious of an unwelcome throbbing that pulsed through her entire body. Alain's grip on her wrist seemed to scorch through her like a bracelet of fire. Then with a low, shuddering sigh he released her. Turning back to the steering-wheel, he switched on the ignition, rammed the car into gear and pulled out on to the road with a protesting squeal of rubber.

'We'll be at Point Cupid in another twenty minutes,' he said with biting sarcasm. 'So you'll soon have the chance to see for yourself whether I've ruined the place or not.'

The streets of Papeete flashed past, ghostlike in the gloom. Down by the harbour, Claire caught a glimpse of the lights of moored ships and heard the distant laughter of all-night revellers on the docks, then Alain took a turning which led out towards the east of the island. Ten minutes later as the car was speeding up a winding road through lush tropical forest, a sudden burst of orange radiance filled the landscape around them.

'Oh, do stop,' begged Claire.

With a brooding glance at her, Alain sent the car hurtling round one final bend and brought the Citroën to a halt in a parking area overlooking the magnificent bay of Point Cupid. Scrambling eagerly out, Claire darted across to the viewing platform and stood gazing out over the ocean. As the sun rose like a blood-red orange from the sea, its rays lit up the dark blue of the outer ocean, the lacy necklace of foam that marked the hidden coral reef and the much lighter blue waters of the lagoon. Down below them a tangle of luxuriant tropical vegetation rioted exuberantly over the hillside. The flaming orange canopies of African tulip trees were noisy with the cries of mynah birds and, further down, coconut palms, hibiscus and banana trees jostled in colourful profusion. Claire gazed and gazed, avidly noting the far-off buildings of Papeete and the yachts at anchor in the harbour.

'You haven't told me what you think of my eyesore of a hotel yet,' reminded a sardonic voice beside her.

'W—what?' stammered Claire. 'Where is it?'

'You're practically on top of it,' said Alain.

Gripping her shoulders, he turned her forty-five degrees further east and pointed downwards. Claire gasped. Tucked into the hillside, so cunningly that it was scarcely visible, was a set of buildings that looked more like a living staircase than a luxury hotel. Built in a series of tiers that followed the shape of the hillside, it was surrounded by coconut palms and banana trees that sheltered it from the wind and the gaze of curious sightseers. In addition, each unit had its own large balcony with planter boxes filled with tropical creepers. Bougainvillaeas in every imaginable shade of scarlet, orange and white cascaded over the walls and the air was heavy with the scent of tropical flowers. On the highest level of the cliff-top, the whole structure was dominated by a longhouse in the traditional Polynesian style, with the graceful swooping lines of a ship's hull. And in the gap between the screen of trees Claire caught a glimpse of the sapphire-blue water of a large swimming-pool.

'It's beautiful,' she acknowledged reluctantly.

Her admission seemed to dissolve some of the hostility between them. Alain's face relaxed into an unexpected smile and he looked almost friendly.

'Why don't you come and have breakfast with me and see it properly?' he invited.

Claire bit her lip.

'I really want to get home and see my family,' she protested.

'Of course,' he agreed. 'But there are some wedding presents for Marie Rose that arrived through my hotel's courier service yesterday. It's some items of china and glassware from my great-aunt in France. She didn't trust them to the mail and I thought you might like to take them with you for your sister.'

'Oh,' said Claire. 'Well, in that case, I suppose I should stop. Besides, nobody ever gets up early in our house. They'll probably all be snoring blissfully if I arrive now.'

'True,' said Alain gravely. 'Besides, there's another reason why you'd be wise to stop here on your way home.'

'What's that?' asked Claire with a puzzled frown.

Alain took her arm and escorted her back to the car.

'According to Marie Rose, your father has been putting in a new bathroom,' he explained.

A horrified look spread over Claire's face.

'Oh, no,' she wailed. 'Papa's been tinkering with the plumbing? You don't mean——?'

'I'm afraid so. Marie Rose says they've had no hot water for the past six weeks, so if you want a decent shower your best chance is at my house. I think you'll find the facilities there are adequate.'

They were more than adequate, they were totally luxurious, Claire discovered. Alain's new house was built at a distance from the main hotel and was set amid such a luxuriant private garden that it seemed totally secluded. White stucco walls and a hedge of red ginger plants almost concealed it from view and, as Alain drove into the double garage, Claire saw that the garden was a riot of colourful tropical plants. Yellow and pink hibiscus flowers jostled for space with cascades of orange and scarlet bougainvillaea that spilt over the enclosing walls. Like the reception building of the hotel, the house was constructed in the traditional Polynesian style with a thatched roof. Yet, as Alain unlocked the front door and led her into the entrance hall, Claire saw that the resemblance to a primitive thatched hut ended there. Once inside, they were met by the discreet hum of airconditioning and a welcome coolness descended on them. Claire gazed around her in surprise, taking in the colourful riot of Polynesian bark paintings, glossy green plants and a glimpse of a vivid, casual living-room with deep, comfortable sofas and bright wall-hangings.

'Goodness,' she murmured under her breath.

'What is it?' demanded Alain.

'I didn't expect your home to look so colourful and relaxed,' admitted Claire, turning to face him.

'Oh?' retorted Alain. 'Why not?'

'It doesn't go with your personality somehow,' explained Claire. 'It's quite different from what I expected.'

'And what did you expect?' he prompted.

Claire wrinkled her nose.

'Oh, white walls, lots of chrome everywhere. A kitchen that looks like a cross between a butcher's shop and an operating theatre. Like that house you were renting a few years ago. The sort of place nobody could really relax in, not that you would worry about that. I mean, you've always been more into working than relaxing, haven't you?'

'I see,' murmured Alain. 'Well, how cosy. It sounds as though you regard me as some kind of clinical, unfeeling robot, whose only interest in life is making money. Am I right?'

Claire's face flamed. She opened her mouth to protest that she hadn't intended anything quite so rude, but saw that Alain was gazing at her with mocking blue eyes that held an unmistakable challenge. Her chin lifted defiantly.

'Yes, I suppose I do,' she replied.

His mouth set grimly and his gaze travelled down over her slender body.

'Well, I won't tell you what sort of decorating style I'd expect you to favour,' he drawled. 'I don't suppose you'd have room to cart soft lighting and red satin sheets around in your little suitcase anyway.'

Claire caught her breath in a sob of rage and her eyes sparkled dangerously. Lunging forward, she tried to wrestle her bag out of his grip.

'How dare you?' she cried unsteadily. 'Look, Alain, I should never have come here! It was ridiculous to think that you and I could be pleasant to each other for five minutes at a time. So, if you'll just call me a taxi, I'll take my unwelcome presence away.'

'Don't be such a melodramatic little fool!' growled Alain. 'You'll go when I'm ready to take you, Claire, and not before. I promised Marie Rose that you and I would get along together until the wedding is over.'

'Fine,' seethed Claire, still trying to wrestle her bag from his grip. 'I'll see you again on the actual day of the wedding and I'll even bare my teeth and smile at you. But in the meantime, give me my suitcase and let me go!'

'When you've had a shower and breakfast and calmed down, I'll let you go!' thundered Alain. 'But I won't allow you to turn up at your home in such a state as this. Your father is a sick man and you'll upset him!'

'I am not in a state!' cried Claire.

'Yes, you are,' contradicted Alain. 'Your hands are shaking! Look at them.'

It was true. Claire looked down and saw that her slim, tanned fingers were gripped around the handle of the bag so tightly that they were trembling. Very slowly and deliberately, as if he were undoing a padlock, Alain prised them free. Then he patted Claire soothingly on the shoulder.

'Now, go and have a shower,' he advised, 'while I order some breakfast for us. You can use the green bedroom through there. And just come back to the dining-room when you're ready.'

Claire stared at him with blazing brown eyes.

'I hate you,' she breathed. 'You're the most over-bearing, ruthless, patronising, hateful——'

'Remember that,' cut in Alain, 'and the next week will pass very smoothly. I'll see you in the dining-room in fifteen minutes, Claire.'

Left alone, Claire stalked into the bedroom, slammed the door and leaned against it, choking for breath.

'Swine!' she muttered. 'Swine, swine, swine!'

But she could see quite clearly that staying in a rage would only serve to amuse Alain even further, so she knew she would have to regain control of herself. Taking a long gulp of air, she looked around her. The room was decorated in cool shades of blue and green and white and the curtains were drawn back, revealing a panoramic view of the ocean. In the far corner was a small sitting area with deep, cream leather armchairs and feathery potted palms, while nearby french doors led on to a private balcony. A queen-sized bed with a colourful floral cover dominated the centre of the room, but there were also spacious built-in wardrobes, a carved chest of drawers and a wall unit that held everything from a tele-

vision set and video-recorder to a large aquarium filled
with red and blue fish. Exploring further, Claire found
a spacious bathroom and let out a low gasp of astonishment at its magnificence. It was faced with palest green
marble and had gold fittings in the shower and bath.
Yet what held her gaze longest was not the décor, but
the view. Because of the house's location high on the
cliff-top, there was no problem of privacy. Consequently
one wall had been lined with huge picture windows,
overlooking the dazzling sapphire vista of the sea.
Walking slowly towards them as if in a dream, Claire
stared down at the beach of black, volcanic sand far
below. Shading her eyes, she peered intently at the cluster
of houses backing on to the foreshore and caught a
glimpse of her parents' modest bungalow between the
coconut palms.

'Oh, it's so nice to be home!' she murmured. 'If only
I didn't have to deal with Alain, everything would be
perfect.'

But she did have to deal with him. That was the whole
problem. If only I hadn't been such a fool six years ago,
she thought passionately, he wouldn't hate me like this!
Still, there's no way I can change the past, so I'll just
have to grit my teeth and get through this somehow...

Five minutes later she was rotating blissfully under
the warm downpour of the shower. In spite of her
tension, a ridiculous, bubbling happiness welled up inside
her each time she remembered she was home. And when
at last she reluctantly turned off the water, wrapped a
gigantic white towel around her and padded into the
bedroom, she did something entirely unexpected.
Reaching down into her suitcase full of neatly folded
clothes, she picked up a smart, tailored black and white
dress and then hesitated. It was an outfit she had worn
several times on reporting assignments and with the small
pearl and gold stud earrings and the black pumps she
knew it made her look cool and sophisticated and totally

in control of life. Exactly the way she wanted to feel in
order to deal with Alain Charpentier. Yet some strange
nostalgia made her replace it in the bag and pick up
something else instead. A dress she hadn't worn for six
years, but which she had never been able to throw away.
A pareu, the national costume of Tahiti, in her favourite
colours of scarlet and white.

Picking up the rectangular piece of cloth, Claire wound
it round her body, tucking it high under her armpits, so
that it concealed her breasts, but left her shoulders bare.
Then, watching herself thoughtfully in the mirror, she
pulled off her plastic shower cap and let her long brown
hair tumble loose to her waist. A jolt of shock went
through her as she saw her own reflection. The last time
she had worn that dress, she had been squirming in Alain
Charpentier's grip, sobbing and pleading and babbling
incoherent explanations as he ordered her to leave Tahiti.
Wearing it now seemed like an act of defiance, a way
of showing him that she could no longer be bullied. If
he even remembered the dress, which was highly unlikely.

Alain's sharp intake of breath as she entered the sitting-
room five minutes later showed her that she was wrong
on that score. His brows drew together in a scowl and
she had no doubt at all that he was remembering the
past just as vividly as she was. However, he made no
mention of it as he rose to his feet and came towards
her.

'You look very attractive,' he said.

'Thank you,' replied Claire warily.

'Let me get you some juice,' suggested Alain. 'I've
ordered breakfast from the hotel, but I don't expect it
for another five minutes or so. Now what would you
like? Orange juice or a tropical medley?'

'Tropical medley, please,' said Claire.

His fingers brushed hers as he handed her the tall,
frosted glass and she flinched. Colouring self-
consciously, she took a hasty gulp of the chilled drink.

It was delicious, thick with shreds of fresh pineapple and mango and full of crushed ice. Alain's gaze did not leave hers as he set down the crystal jug on the coffee-table.

'Well, sit down and tell me about yourself,' he ordered abruptly. 'How did you get into this television reporting in the first place? Was it your little brush with the film world in Tahiti that inspired you?'

Claire cast him a suspicious glance, but was not certain whether any malice lay behind his question. In any case, she decided that dignity was her best defence. Sitting back in her chair and toying with her glass, she adopted the cool, poised manner that had seen her through countless difficult interviews.

'No, not at all,' she replied. 'It was pure chance really. After I left home, I went to stay with relatives in Sydney. As you probably know, my mother is originally Australian and she had always planned for me to spend a year in Australia when I finished school. Anyway my aunt managed to find me a job at a television station as a sort of Girl Friday. In the beginning I was only doing odd jobs, typing, making coffee, running messages, that sort of thing. But then I had a lucky break.'

'What happened?' he asked.

'A famous French scientist from New Caledonia was visiting Sydney and we had a reporter who spoke French lined up to do a live interview with him. But as they were all coming down the stairs to the recording studio, the reporter slipped and broke his ankle. Of course, there was instant pandemonium. The poor chap was in dreadful pain and couldn't possibly go on air, but the interview was due to start at any moment. I was the only other person around who spoke fluent French, so I offered to do it. Luckily the head of the studio was very impressed with the result.'

'And so?' prompted Alain.

Claire smiled.

'And so nothing,' she retorted with a shrug. 'For the next few months, everything went on exactly as usual, but then one day the boss called me into his office. He said they were starting up a new programme about international scientific discoveries and they wanted a roving reporter who spoke a major language other than English. He offered me the job on a trial basis and naturally I jumped at the chance.'

'And you enjoy it, do you?' asked Alain, eyeing her searchingly.

Claire sighed.

'I did at first,' she agreed. 'What twenty-year-old wouldn't? Constantly jetting around the world, wearing lovely clothes, having somebody else do my hair and my make-up every day. Yes, it's been fun! But it's also a lot harder than it looks. Lately I've found the constant travel an absolute nightmare and I'm not alone in that. None of the other original team of reporters is still doing the job. The others all found it clashed too much with their family commitments and gave it up.'

'But you didn't have that problem?' asked Alain with a touch of sarcasm.

'No,' replied Claire shortly. 'As you say, I didn't have that problem. All the same, I sometimes find myself at some ungodly hour of the morning waiting for a change of planes in Singapore airport and feeling dead on my feet. And I ask myself, "What on earth am I doing this for?"'

'I know what you mean,' agreed Alain, staring out of the window with a brooding expression. 'I've almost worked myself to death trying to get these new hotels up and running, but I don't know if there's really any point to it. Perhaps if I had someone to share it with, I might feel differently.'

'You've never thought about marrying?' asked Claire curiously.

Alain's mouth tightened. Setting down his glass, he strode across to the huge picture window and stared sombrely out to sea.

'Only once,' he replied indifferently. 'There was only one girl who ever touched my heart. But it soon became apparent that my good opinion of her was totally unfounded. So why bother? If I were going to marry, I would want a wife whom I could trust completely. A woman who would commit herself to me, body and soul. Not an easy thing to find these days!'

'Don't be so cynical!' protested Claire. 'There are plenty of women like that!'

Alain swung round to face her, his blue eyes glittering fiercely.

'Are there?' he sneered.

Claire flinched at the bitterness in his tone. It was as if he felt that no woman could be trusted because a single person had once betrayed him.

'I think you're being absurd,' she said with spirit. 'You shouldn't let one bad experience sour your entire life. Anyway, what about all the women you go around with? Don't they mean anything to you?'

Alain's eyes narrowed.

'What do you know of the women I go around with?' he demanded.

Claire flushed.

'Only what Marie Rose tells me,' she muttered.

'I see,' said Alain thoughtfully. 'So you find my private life interesting enough to ask Marie Rose about it, do you?'

'No!' cried Claire. 'I didn't do anything of the kind, but you know what Marie Rose is like. Her biggest interest in life is other people's relationships. If she could pair off everybody she knows and march them up the ramp to Noah's Ark, she'd die happy! Anyway, whenever I phone home, she always tells me about everybody's love life. Yours included.'

Alain swore under his breath.

'If I didn't need Marie Rose in my new hotel, I'd wring her neck for her impertinence!' he vowed. 'But if Marie Rose keeps you so well informed, you must realise that there have been women who were only too happy to join me for a frolic in a tropical paradise. Women who meant as much to me as I meant to them. Which was absolutely nothing! And I dare say that will be the pattern for the rest of my life.'

Claire stared at him in dismay.

'I think that's awful,' she said bluntly.

'Do you?' retorted Alain. 'How odd. I thought you were the expert when it came to sexual frolics without commitment.'

With an angry gasp Claire shot to her feet, knocking over her glass of juice.

'How can you be so——?' she began.

But at that moment the front door bell chimed musically. Alain strode off to answer it and Claire was left fuming.

'Come in, Paulette,' invited Alain.

A moment later the door to the sitting-room opened and an elderly Tahitian woman dressed in a scarlet pareu with a garland of acacia blossoms in her hair came in with a heavy tray in her hands. She smiled dazzlingly at Claire and wished her good morning before trudging through into the dining-room.

'There you are, Monsieur Alain,' she said, setting down the tray. 'Juice, croissants, butter, jam and fresh coffee from the hotel restaurant. Is there anything else I can bring you?'

'No, thank you, Paulette,' replied Alain pleasantly. 'But if you could just mop up the couch I'd be grateful. Mademoiselle Beaumont had an accident with her drink.'

'*Ooh, là!*' exclaimed the housekeeper, clicking her tongue. 'But, of course, *monsieur*. I'll just fetch a cloth from your kitchen.'

Paulette was stoutly built and Claire felt a pang of guilt as she saw the older woman waddle back and sink to her knees with the damp cloth.

'Oh, let me,' she begged. 'It was my fault.'

'But of course not, *mademoiselle*,' protested Paulette in outrage. 'This is my job. You sit down and enjoy your breakfast. *Ta maa maitai*. Good appetite.'

'*Mauruuru*,' replied Claire. 'Thank you.'

The task did not take long and, in spite of the maid's protests, Claire stood by and helped her to her feet when she finished.

'You're very kind, mademoiselle,' Paulette panted. 'Thank you very much.'

'*Aita pea pea*,' smiled Claire. 'No problem.'

As the front door finally closed behind the older woman, Alain gave Claire a long, piercing look.

'That was considerate of you,' he said in a faintly puzzled tone.

Claire returned his gaze with undisguised resentment.

'You sound as if that surprises you,' she remarked.

'It does,' agreed Alain bluntly. 'But never mind that now. Come and sit down before the coffee gets cold.'

In spite of her annoyance Claire joined him at the table and was soon enjoying an excellent breakfast. The croissants were warm and flaky and rich with butter, the raspberry jam was deliciously fruity and the hot coffee was fragrant and reviving. As they ate Alain began to talk about his new hotel on Moorea where Marie Rose would be living after the wedding and Claire found herself listening with unexpected interest.

'It sounds heavenly,' she admitted. 'And, of course, we've heaps of cousins on Moorea, so Marie Rose certainly won't feel lonely when she moves.'

'You're fortunate to have such a close family,' remarked Alain. 'I suppose you've missed them while you were away.'

'Yes,' replied Claire. 'Of course, it was rather a blow when my grandfather died last year.'

Her face shadowed at the thought. A severe ear infection had made flying impossible for her at the time, so she had not even been able to attend his funeral. That was one occasion when even the risk of meeting Alain would not have kept her away from the island. As it was, she had spent the day of her grandfather's funeral in tears, finding her exile more painful than ever.

'I was sorry to hear about it,' said Alain.

'Oh, well,' continued Claire, shaking her head. 'He had a very happy life and lived to be eighty-one. It would be wrong to mourn him.'

'He was French originally, wasn't he?' asked Alain.

'Yes,' replied Claire, brightening suddenly. 'He came out to Tahiti to do his military service, fell in love with a local girl and lived happily ever after. Rather a romantic story, really. Although very common in the islands, of course.'

'I'm not so sure about that,' replied Alain. 'Not every Frenchman who falls in love with a Tahitian girl manages to live happily ever after.'

Claire winced at the bitterness in his tone. Was Alain talking about himself? she wondered. But before she could say anything, he continued abruptly.

'And your parents?' he quizzed. 'Do you think they're happy?'

Claire frowned thoughtfully.

'I think so,' she said. 'Although Papa does have some health problems now. But he has a new business venture going too and he seems very pleased about that. He's taking four-wheel-drive tours to the interior of the island. I don't know if you've heard about them.'

'Yes, I have,' said Alain. 'Many of the guests at my hotels have been going on them. They've been very popular. My sister Louise went on one when she was here last year.'

There was a sudden deathly silence and Claire's coffee-spoon clattered loudly off the saucer and fell to the floor. For a moment she sat rigid, feeling as sick and shocked as if she were about to faint, then she bent down to retrieve it. But Alain was ahead of her, his fingers closing over the silverware before she could even reach it.

'You look very pale,' he said deliberately as they both straightened up. 'Does the thought of my sister really upset you so much?'

Claire stared at him with a stricken expression, but his face was as cruel and pitiless as a Spanish inquisitor's. His blue eyes seared through her like jets of flame.

'Well?' he taunted.

She drew in a long, agonised breath.

'I asked you a question!' he shouted, slamming his open hand on the table.

Claire leapt to her feet, feeling her legs shake beneath her, but she stared back at him defiantly. Then she let out her breath in a ragged gasp.

'Yes,' she whispered. 'It upsets me.'

Suddenly Alain too was on his feet, staring at her across the barrier of the table.

'Oh?' he challenged. 'Really? It didn't upset you six years ago though, did it?'

'That's not true!' cried Claire.

She broke away, felt tears stinging her eyes and stumbled across to the window. Relentlessly Alain pursued her and his powerful hand closed on her wrist.

'Isn't it?' he insisted, hauling her up against him, so that she could feel the tension in his hard, muscular body. 'Well, if thinking about Louise upset you, it was never obvious. It didn't stop you from going to bed with her husband, did it?'

'Stop it!' cried Claire wildly.

Snatching herself free from Alain's grip, she covered her face with her hands. A violent shudder went through her. But Alain was totally merciless. Seizing her hands, he pulled them away and glared down at her. He was so close that she could feel his swift, thudding heartbeat through his thin shirt, smell the spicy odour of his cologne, see the muscle twitching in his left temple.

'You didn't care how much you hurt Louise, did you?' he insisted savagely. 'Did you? All you wanted was to have a wild roll in the hay with Marcel and to hell with the consequences!'

'That's not true!' protested Claire.

'Isn't it?' sneered Alain. 'You seem to forget that I found you in bed with him in my own house, you lying little schemer!'

Claire's face flamed.

'I haven't forgotten,' she choked.

'Neither have I!' growled Alain. 'Every detail of that day is burnt into my mind like acid and I wish to God it weren't. Because then I wouldn't have to recognise you for the heartless, destructive troublemaker that you are.'

'You're being totally unfair!' cried Claire.

Alain gave a harsh laugh and thrust her aside contemptuously. Striding across the room, he came to a halt and turned on her with uncontrolled vehemence.

'Am I?' he demanded. 'So you deny that I found you naked in my own bed with Marcel, do you?'

Claire let out a low groan.

'No, I don't!' she cried. 'How can I? You know perfectly well that it's true, but you're still being unfair, Alain! I didn't know that Marcel was married, I swear to God I didn't! I never even knew that Louise existed.'

'I'm sure!' jeered Alain disbelievingly.

'Look,' insisted Claire, 'whatever you say, that's the truth, Alain! And you couldn't possibly feel worse about what happened than I did. But I never intended to hurt anybody. You know what Marcel was like as well as I do—handsome, glamorous and full of charm. And a film director into the bargain. And I was nineteen years old and very, very gullible. I believed him when he told me he was in love with me, I even believed him when he said he wanted to marry me. But he certainly never told me he had a wife already tucked away in Paris!'

Alain's only response was an incredulous lift of the eyebrows. That small, contemptuous gesture goaded Claire into action. With an inarticulate cry, she flung herself at him and seized him by the arms.

'It's the truth!' she cried. 'You must believe me, Alain!'

Her impetuous rush caught him off balance and almost sent them both toppling. Instinctively he reached out to steady her and she found herself imprisoned in those hard, unyielding arms. She gave a low, distraught gasp and her body quivered under his touch. Her involuntary movement sparked an unexpected response in Alain. For a moment he stared down at her, his blue eyes glazed with anger, or possibly something else. Then, like some savage bird of prey, he suddenly swooped.

Claire uttered a startled squeak as his mouth came down on hers in the fiercest and most enthralling kiss she had ever experienced in her life. For an instant she stood rigid with shock, then molten fire seemed to flow through her veins as Alain took violent possession of her mouth. There was a strange roaring in her ears and she felt dizzy with longing as his hard, urgent fingers traced sensual patterns on her back. His ferocity woke an answering urgency in her and without any conscious intent she kissed him back with equal force. His male strength was warm and insistent against her and she was shocked to hear the soft, whimpering sounds that rose in her throat as she let herself lean wantonly against him. Time lost all meaning as they swayed in that warm, pulsing embrace. Then suddenly Alain thrust her furiously away from him.

'You haven't changed!' he exclaimed bitterly. 'You're still throwing yourself at men without thought for the consequences, aren't you, Claire?'

The unfairness of it took her breath away. She stood staring at him with her shoulders heaving and her mouth gaping open. Then suddenly she regained her voice.

'You swine!' she breathed. 'There's no possible way I can get along with you for the next week. No way on earth!'

CHAPTER TWO

As THE gleaming Citroën turned into the road leading to Acajou Beach, Claire leaned eagerly forward to catch the first glimpse of her parents' house. For the present even her hostility towards Alain was forgotten as she scanned the dense thickets of scarlet bougainvillaea, yellow hibiscus and flapping green banana trees that hid most of the houses from view. Then, as they neared the last few buildings near the turquoise water, she let out a low cry of delight.

'That's it!'

Like Alain's house, it had a hedge of red ginger plants in the front garden, but there the resemblance ended. While the Beaumonts' home might be casual and welcoming, it was undoubtedly rather shabby. The paint was peeling, weeds grew almost as profusely as flowers around the boundary fence and there was a large rusty bath sitting like a wrecked ship on the front lawn. Claire felt herself tensing uncomfortably as Alain turned into the uneven driveway. It was bad enough that he disapproved of her so violently, without the added humiliation of having him despise her home and family. She could only hope that he would drop her off quickly and make his departure. Unfortunately Alain did nothing of the kind.

As the car came to halt, there was a sudden flurry of activity from within the house. Marie Rose, a large, buxom girl with a resonant voice, burst out of the front door, shrieking joyfully 'They're here! They're here!' She was almost tripped up by a tan-coloured mongrel of doubtful parentage that surged down the steps, yelping

31

wildly, and hurtled towards Claire like a prize steeple-chaser. There was an outburst of hugs and kisses, barks and licks.

'Oh, Claire, it's so good to see you!' cried Marie Rose. 'I'm sorry Paul couldn't be here. There are some problems with the new hotel buildings on Moorea, but you'll meet him tomorrow. Oh, I've got so much to tell you!'

From inside the house there was the sound of slamming doors and more hurrying footsteps. Then suddenly Claire found herself in the midst of a human—and animal—throng with everyone talking at once and hugging her warmly, while the dog pirouetted around like a demented ballerina. When at last she was able to draw breath, she tidied her hair with one hand and held down the lunging family pet with the other.

'Oh, it's so good to see you all!' she cried. 'You can't imagine how I've missed you.'

'We've missed you too,' a little girl without any front teeth assured her earnestly. 'But I've missed you the most of all, because I've never even met you!'

That made everybody laugh and Claire was quick to fall to her knees to give the child another hug.

'Then you must be my cousin Nicole,' she said. 'And it's very nice to meet you at last.'

'It's nice to meet you too,' agreed Nicole pertly. 'And we're having barbecued pig for dinner because you've come home. A whole pig!'

'Cooked the traditional way in a pit,' agreed Claire's father. 'Just the way you always liked it best, *chérie*.'

His hands rested warmly on Claire's shoulders and he smiled down at her. She felt an uncomfortable tremor of emotion pass through her as she looked up at him. For there were so many coils of silver in Roland Beaumont's hair, so many extra wrinkles that hadn't been there when she left home. And, although he was still as massive and powerfully built as ever, the faint bluish

tinge around his lips and the slight wheeze when he
breathed, alarmed her considerably.

'Oh, Papa!' she exclaimed with a catch in her voice.
'How kind of you! Thank you.'

'You will stay and help us eat it, won't you, Alain?'
continued Roland as warmly as if Alain were a member
of the family. 'You'll be very welcome.'

'But Papa!' protested Claire. 'I just wanted a quiet
family gathering.'

A sudden hush fell on the group and Claire was instantly conscious of her father's frown and her mother's
horrified pantomime of disapproval. Realising how rude
she had sounded, she stammered a reluctant apology.

'S-sorry. I didn't mean it quite like that. It's just that
I'm exhausted from the flight and I'm sure Alain has
better things to do. Although naturally I'd be delighted
if he would stay.'

She fixed her gaze steadily on Alain, willing him to
decline. But his blue eyes met hers with cruel amusement
and a small, taunting smile played around the corners
of his mouth.

'Well, if you'd be delighted for me to stay, Claire,' he
murmured, 'I can hardly refuse, can I? Thank you very
much for the invitation.'

As Claire's mother ushered them all into the house,
she gave her elder daughter a warning look.

'I'll just help Claire get settled in her room,' she said
brightly. 'Then we'll all come out on the patio and have
a drink together.'

The moment the bedroom door had closed behind
them, Eve Beaumont shook her head in dismay.

'Whatever came over you, Claire?' she demanded.
'How could you make Alain feel so unwelcome? What
a dreadful thing to do, especially when he's been so good
and kind to us!'

'What do you mean, good and kind?' muttered Claire.

Eve sighed. Watching her closely, Claire saw that her mother's blonde hair was fading imperceptibly to silver and that there were lines of strain around her mouth.

'Well, he and Marie Rose's fiancé are like brothers,' she explained. 'And even though we haven't seen much of Alain, he's always been very kind when we have had dealings with him. Nothing is ever too much trouble for him. You know I don't drive and he's been wonderful about taking your father to the hospital for his medical check-ups. And when your Papa was too sick to take a four-wheel-drive tour into the mountains, Alain arranged for a substitute driver for two weeks and wouldn't accept any payment for it. So I think the least you can do is be polite to him.'

Claire bit her lip guiltily. However much she might resent Alain herself, the quarrel certainly had nothing to do with the rest of her family. Setting down her bag, she gave her mother a quick, awkward hug.

'I'm sorry,' she said with more sincerity than she had shown earlier. 'I didn't mean to cause trouble and I promise I'll be nice to Alain.'

'That's my girl!' replied Eve, catching her in a warm embrace. 'Now, come on, let's go out and see if we can produce a decent party!'

By lunchtime everyone agreed that they were producing a very decent party. A homecoming was always a good excuse for celebrating in style and nobody in Tahiti was ever foolish enough to rush a celebration. Here in the islands nearly everybody lived in large, extended families and a daughter's homecoming was a big occasion. Two sets of aunts and uncles, half a dozen cousins, all the neighbours on the block and ten or twelve of Claire's old schoolfriends provided a good basis for a guest list. And, since nobody arrived empty-handed, there was plenty to eat and drink while they waited for the pig to finish cooking. By noon there was a dull roar of conversation, counterpointed by children's laughter, the clink of ice-cubes in glasses, some lively ukelele music and the faint rustle of banana leaves in the tropical breeze. Overhead white puffs of cloud drifted lazily in a soft, blue sky and beyond the wall the lagoon glittered jade-green under the midday sun. It was impossible to go on feeling tense in such a setting.

Claire, who had been temporarily deserted by her affectionate clan, closed her eyes and let herself relax in a deck chair on the patio. It felt marvellous to enjoy the steady warmth of the sun beating down on her bare arms, the scent of flowers and salt air and the distant swish, swish of the waves lapping on the sand...until the scrape of another chair on the paving bricks intruded on her reverie. Her eyes flew open.

'Oh, it's you,' she said bleakly.

Alain gave a short laugh.

'Don't sound so overjoyed,' he warned. 'I might feel tempted to stay and chat.'

This sarcasm made Claire bristle and yet she could not help noticing the smoky, rather hoarse quality of his voice. As a teenager she had found it unbearably seductive, but now it filled her with panic. In any other man she would have thought it very attractive, but not in Alain Charpentier.

'What do you want?' she demanded, sitting rigidly upright as she watched him move the chairs and peer underneath.

'A pair of canvas gardening gloves,' he replied. 'Your father assures me that he left them somewhere over here. I need them to help lift the pig out of the pit.'

But a joint search beneath the deck chairs and around the pot plants that bordered the patio failed to locate the missing gloves.

'Try the flowerbed near the African tulip tree,' suggested Claire. 'Unless Papa has changed dramatically, he's probably left them out there when he got sick of weeding. Over there, see? Where the women are setting up the tables.'

Alain's gaze followed her pointing finger to the spot where a group of chattering, laughing women were leisurely draping tablecloths and arranging dishes on a battered collection of garden furniture.

'Why aren't you helping them?' he asked.

Claire stiffened, wondering whether he was attacking her. Then she remembered her promise to her mother. She was going to be nice to Alain Charpentier, even if it killed her.

'I was helping,' she protested. 'But I dropped a glass bowl of green salad and they decided I was more trouble than I was worth.'

'Understandable,' said Alain tersely. 'I've often thought the same thing about you myself.'

Claire ground her teeth.

'I can't do a thing right where you're concerned, can I?' she demanded. 'You've simply made up your mind that I'm selfish and that's that!'

'If the cap fits...' murmured Alain.

'You're impossible!' snapped Claire.

As they stood staring at each other in angry confrontation, Marie Rose appeared around the corner of the house. Her gaze darted from Alain's grimly set jaw to Claire's flushed cheeks.

'Whatever's going on?' she asked in dismay.

'Nothing important,' muttered Claire, tossing her head and turning pointedly away from Alain. 'Did you want something, Marie Rose?'

'Yes—Alain. The other men are ready to lift the pig now and they want him to come and help.'

'I couldn't find the gloves,' confessed Alain.

'No problem,' replied Marie Rose, brandishing them triumphantly. 'Papa had left them in the flowerbed under the tulip tree, so we're all organised now. Don't you want to come and watch, Claire?'

'All right,' agreed Claire in a subdued voice.

She was so angry with Alain that she would gladly have climbed over the boundary wall and marched off along the beach without a backward glance, but such an action was unthinkable. After all, she was the guest of honour and the raising of the pig was the highlight of traditional Tahitian barbecue. So she followed her sister across the garden with no more than a single resentful glance at Alain. And when they stood on the edge of the smoking pit she watched with interest while the huge parcel was lifted carefully out and laid on a metal tray. Once the banana leaves were unwrapped, the smell of succulent barbecued pork filled the air.

'Try a piece, Claire,' urged her father.

'Mmm. Wonderful,' she approved, licking her fingers. 'Even better than usual. Did you put something special in the marinade?'

'Alain did,' replied Roland. 'It's his recipe, so you'll have to ask him if you want the secret.'

Alain. Always, Alain, thought Claire, with a flash of resentment. Can't this family do anything without him these days? But she tried not to let any sign of her annoyance show in her face as she watched Alain carving the pork. All the same, she was conscious of Marie Rose watching her with a troubled expression. Forcing herself to smile, Claire looked across at her sister.

'It's a wonderful party, Marie Rose,' she said. 'I hope you didn't spend days and days getting it all ready.'

'I was happy to do it,' replied Marie Rose. 'I only hope you're going to enjoy your stay here.'

There was such a worried note in her voice that Claire could have kicked herself. Poor Marie Rose! How typical of her to spend days preparing a welcome home party for Claire at a time when she was so busy. And how ungrateful it would be if Claire didn't make any effort to enjoy herself! With that thought firmly in mind, Claire took her laden plate and sat at a table under the big tulip

tree. She was soon deep in sparkling conversation with
two of her cousins.

The meal was excellent and reflected the rich cultural
diversity of Tahiti. Apart from the traditional Polynesian
spread of barbecued pork, breadfruit, steamed yams and
bland, porridge-like *poi*, there was a tempting array of
other dishes. The Chungs, who lived across the road,
had brought Chinese beef in black bean sauce on a bed
of rice and crisp, stir-fried vegetables. And there were
yards of crusty French bread, various chicken cas-
seroles, salads and huge platters of luscious mangoes,
pineapple and bananas. Finally, as a triumphant conclusion to the meal, Eve Beaumont cooked a huge pile
of pancakes, doused them in Grand Marnier liqueur and
set them alight. When the blue flames had finally died
down everybody crowded around to eat the crisp, hot,
syrupy crêpes. After that, people lay down under the
coconut palms and rested while Roland played the
ukulele.

The long, lazy afternoon wore on and at sunset Claire's
cousins brought out their tall wooden drums covered in
shark skin and began to beat them, softly at first and
then with rising excitement. Soon everybody was dancing
the *tamure*, shaking their hips, clapping their knees and
uttering shrill cries of excitement. For the first time Claire
felt her tension ebb away from her completely and she
kicked off her light sandals and joined the dancers.
Conscious only of the compulsive rhythm of the drums,
she let herself plunge into the movements of the dance
and gave it all she had. Claire had always been an excellent dancer. Slim, lithe and graceful with boundless
energy, she was soon vibrating joyously over the trampled
sand. One by one the other dancers came to a halt and
backed away. Claire was vaguely conscious that they had
drifted away, but she did not pause to wonder why. The
drums were still thudding urgently and that was enough
to keep her hips shimmering at the speed of light and

her arms swaying gracefully, while she called the traditional cries. Only when the frenzied drumbeat stopped and she slowed to a halt, gasping and laughing, did she realise that everyone was watching her. For a moment she stood still in confusion, then suddenly her cousin Pierre clapped his hands together sharply. A thunder of applause followed and her friends and neighbours gathered around, patting her on the back and admiring her skill.

'You should stay and join our dancing troupe for the Bastille Day celebrations,' said one of her friends. 'We'd probably win the Heiva I Tahiti competition if we had you in our group.'

There were cries of agreement and other voices took up the plea. Then Alain Charpentier's voice sounded chill and clear through the warm hubbub of their admiration.

'Bastille Day is not until the fourteenth of July,' he pointed out. 'That's well over a month away. Claire will have to go home to Australia and her job long before that.'

Claire's head jerked up and she stared at him. He was standing under a coconut palm with his back to the blazing sunset, so she could not see his features clearly. But the red gleam of the dying sun outlined his taut, muscular body and revealed the tension in his stance. His arms were folded and his chin had an arrogant, challenging tilt to it. An obscure pain stabbed through her at his words. Not only because of the antagonism they revealed, but because of their substance. Alain was right. She would have to be back in Australia long before Bastille Day. Although it would never seem like home to her.

'Well, we'll have to see, won't we?' she said sweetly, resenting Alain's obvious desire to be rid of her. 'Perhaps I could get longer holiday leave from the TV station. Or perhaps I'll decide to move back to Tahiti permanently. Who knows?'

She saw Alain's fingers tighten convulsively on his folded arms at that, but he said nothing. And shortly afterwards the party broke up. An hour or so was spent tidying up and chatting to her parents, then the moment Claire had been dreading finally arrived. The moment when she found herself alone with Marie Rose.

Her sister was nothing if not direct. Kicking the door of their shared bedroom shut, Marie Rose flung herself down on one of the beds and fixed Claire with a piercing gaze.

'Have you and Alain quarrelled already?' she demanded.

Claire gave a weary sigh, sat down on the other bed and began to undress.

'Oh, for heaven's sake!' she protested. 'I was flying all night, Marie Rose, first from Australia to New Zealand and then to Tahiti. And I've just enjoyed an eight-hour party. I'm tired!'

She flung her clothes down in a heap, pulled on a nightdress and huddled into bed.

'Not too tired to answer me,' insisted Marie Rose, sitting on Claire's bed and snatching the covers with a deft swoop. 'Come on, big sister. Just answer a few painless questions and I promise you can have your sheets back.'

'Beast!' cried Claire, snatching wildly.

There was a sharp, ripping sound and they stared at each other in dismay, like two naughty children.

'Now look what you've made me do!' said Claire crossly.

Marie Rose gave a sudden, explosive giggle. Claire glared at her for a moment, then her gravity dissolved. The two of them lay hooting helplessly with laughter as if they were ten years old again. Then Claire hauled herself up against her pillows, arranged the mangled sheets around her and stared at her sister. Perhaps it was better to get the ordeal over with.

'All right, what do you want to know?' she demanded warily.

Marie Rose's dancing brown eyes sobered suddenly.

'Have you and Alain quarrelled?' she asked.

'Yes,' said Claire curtly.

'But why?' persisted Marie Rose.

'Because he hates me!' flared Claire. 'And he makes no secret of the fact.'

'That's not true,' replied Marie Rose. 'I'm sure it's not! I would never have asked him to meet you at the airport if I'd thought that.'

Claire huddled her legs into a mound and clasped her arms defensively around her knees.

'Why did you ask him anyway?' she demanded. 'That was one of the nastiest shocks I've had for a long time, being met by him.'

Marie Rose climbed to her feet and paced across the room with a guilty expression.

'I'm sorry,' she said. 'I know you took a dislike to him years ago before you left for Australia, but I've never understood why. After all, you used to worship the ground he walked on.'

'More fool me,' exclaimed Claire tartly.

Marie Rose sighed.

'But what went wrong between you?' she demanded. 'What did he do to offend you?'

Claire's eyes took on a haunted look.

'That's my business and I'm not prepared to discuss it.'

'Well, there you are!' exclaimed Marie Rose. 'I knew you'd probably refuse to come to the wedding if you knew he was the best man. And I couldn't bear to get married without you, so I didn't tell you before you left Sydney. Anyway, I hoped that if I sent Alain to meet you somehow you'd smooth things over between you.'

Claire snorted derisively.

'Some chance!' she exclaimed. 'Especially when he loathes the sight of me.'

Marie Rose sank down on her own bed and stared at Claire in dismay.

'You keep saying that,' she protested. 'But I'm sure it's not true. Whenever Alain comes over here, he always asks if there's any news of you and his eyes take on a kind of brooding look. I've always suspected that he was secretly in love with you.'

'In love with me?' echoed Claire. 'Don't be ridiculous.'

'It's not ridiculous!' insisted Marie Rose. 'Don't you remember six years ago when he first came to Tahiti and Papa had that restaurant down on the beach below Point Cupid? Alain used to come in every day for lunch. I'm sure it's because you were working as a waitress there.'

'More likely because he enjoyed Papa's cooking,' said Claire sceptically.

'I don't think it was only that,' objected Marie Rose. 'His face used to light up whenever he saw you.'

Claire's eyes took on a faraway look as she thought of those long-ago days at her father's short-lived restaurant. Yes, Alain had come in nearly every day for lunch. But had his face really lit up when he saw her or was that just more of Marie Rose's imaginative fervour at work? Struggle as she might, Claire found herself unable to remember anything clearly except for the embarassing schoolgirl crush that she had had on Alain. Every time she had gone near him, she had blushed with embarrassment. Yet Alain had certainly not seemed to return her interest. In fact, he had always struck her as rather stern and disapproving of the girlish giggles that sometimes issued from the kitchen. It was true that his brooding blue eyes had sometimes seemed to follow her around the dining area, but only until his meal arrived. And his rare and unexpectedly charming smiles had always been accompanied by some quite trivial remark about the food. Anyway, if he had loved her, wouldn't

he have listened to her version of what had happened
with Marcel?

Her thoughts went back to the smooth-talking,
handsome Frenchman who had lured her into his em-
braces six years earlier. Where Alain had seemed like an
unattainable dream, Marcel had been all too ready to
share Claire's company. It had begun innocently enough
with a chance meeting on Marcel's yacht in the harbour,
progressed through picnics and visits to discos and cul-
minated in that appalling scene in Alain's house, which
she could not remember without a shudder. At the time
it had all seemed perfectly harmless. Marcel had announced that his brother-in-law had gone to Paris for
two weeks and asked Marcel to look after his house.
What could be more natural than for him to invite Claire
to lunch? She had gone quite trustingly, never guessing
that she would be plied with far more wine than she was
used to drinking. Never guessing either that Marcel's
brother-in-law would return home early and discover
them together. It had been the final irony to learn that
Alain was Marcel's brother-in-law. And that he was not,
as Claire had supposed, Marcel's sister's husband, but
his wife's brother. She winced at the memory.

'Are you all right?' asked Marie Rose. 'You look pale.'

'It's nothing,' replied Claire in a strained voice. 'I was
just thinking that you're wrong about Alain. He doesn't
even like me. We had a quarrel years ago and he's never
forgiven me.'

'A quarrel?' prompted Marie Rose. 'When? What
about?'

Claire bit her lip. For a moment she was tempted to
blurt out the whole truth to her sister. She knew Marie
Rose would not blame her for what had happened, but
Claire had never found it easy to confide her deepest
feelings to anyone. And she had a strong suspicion that
she would simply break down and howl if she talked

about it. Anyway, it was a long time ago and best forgotten.

'Nothing important,' she lied. 'It was just before I left for Aunt Susan's. That's what made me bring the trip forward a month, actually.'

'Was it about another man?' demanded Marie Rose shrewdly.

Claire squirmed.

'Sort of,' she admitted.

Marie Rose smiled triumphantly.

'Then Alain was probably jealous!' she exclaimed.

'Jealous?' snorted Claire.

'Yes. You shouldn't be fooled by that cool exterior, you know. Alain's a lot like you really, Claire. He bottles things up and smoulders over them and, when he finally does explode, watch out! I've worked for him and I should know. Most of the time he's completely charming and very considerate, but there's no denying he's got a hell of a temper. All the same, he's incredibly sexy, isn't he? If I were you, I'd really make a play for him.'

'Don't be ridiculous!' protested Claire. 'He doesn't even like me.'

'Then why did he take you to his place instead of bringing you straight home this morning?' asked Marie Rose.

'To pick up your china that Aunt Someone or Other had sent you from France,' replied Claire irritably. 'Didn't he give it to you?'

'Yes, he did. But that was just an excuse, any fool could see it. He took you there because he wanted to talk to you. Obviously.'

'Oh. Obviously,' agreed Claire with heavy sarcasm. 'Or quarrel with me, as the case may be. After all, he could hardly shout at me in the airport, could he? Or kiss me,' she added unwisely.

Marie Rose's eyes widened.

'Wow!' she said, leaning forward with the sort of absorbed expression she usually reserved for her favourite soap operas. 'He must really have it bad, Claire! What happened then? Did he tell you he loved you or anything?'

'Oh, stop it!' cried Claire impatiently. 'He wasn't kissing me as if he loved me, Marie Rose, but as if he hated me. Almost as if he were doing it against his will.'

Marie Rose lay back on her bed, hugging her pillow, and sighed ecstatically.

'I think that's the most romantic thing I've ever heard of,' she murmured. 'I'll bet it was earth-shaking when he kissed you, wasn't it?'

'Oh, do shut up and go to sleep!' begged Claire, instantly regretting her impulsive admission.

'All right,' yawned Marie Rose, dropping the subject with surprising readiness. 'Listen, one more thing. Are you really thinking of chucking in your TV job and staying in Tahiti or did you only say that to annoy Alain?'

'I don't know,' replied Claire wearily. 'I'm tempted, Rosie. I didn't realise just how homesick I was until now. But I couldn't stay here if I felt Alain was going to keep up this feud with me. Now go to sleep, will you?'

Marie Rose smirked.

'All right. On one condition.'

'What's that?' asked Claire.

'That you come across to Moorea with me tomorrow. I've promised to take Paul's parents over and show them the hotel, but I'm really dreading it. His father's nice enough, but his mother seems to think they're doing me a tremendous honour by allowing me to marry into the family. And they've got this dreadful woman staying with them who'll be coming to the wedding. Nadine Hugo. I'll need a bit of moral support to cope with her, I can tell you.'

Claire grinned as she turned out the light.

'OK,' she agreed. 'What are bridesmaids for, after all?
I'll entertain the ogress for you.'

In spite of Marie Rose's dire warnings, Claire was in
high spirits as she prepared breakfast the following
morning. She couldn't wait to visit the island of Moorea
again and surely the mysterious Nadine couldn't be as
bad as all that? Well, at least Marie Rose hadn't asked
her to entertain Alain Charpentier for the day! That
would really be stretching loyalty too far. Humming, she
popped a plate of croissants into the microwave oven
and waited for the timer to ring. As she did so, she heard
her father's heavy footsteps behind her.

'Hello, *chérie*,' he rumbled cheerfully, kissing her
cheek. 'Any plans for today?'

'Yes. Marie Rose and I are going to Moorea so that
I can meet Paul and see where she's going to live after
the wedding.'

'Good idea,' said Roland, sinking into a chair. 'I'll
give you both a ride to the ferry. I have to pick up a
party of tourists from a hotel near the wharf at nine
o'clock anyway.'

'Nine o'clock?' teased Claire. 'Whatever's come over
you, Papa? I've never known you get out of bed before
midday before!'

Roland sighed heavily and shook his head.

'Ah. *Aita maita'i*,' he muttered. 'No good, Claire. It's
no laughing matter. If I'd been a better father to you
and worked harder in the past, I'd have more to leave
you now. But what's to become of you if something
happens to me, eh? Answer me that.'

A cold chill of alarm took hold of Claire. She had
never known her father be anything but cheerful before
and his words upset her. But she pushed her foreboding
resolutely away.

'Don't be silly,' she protested, dropping a kiss lightly
on his cheek. 'Nothing's going to happen to you, Papa.

Now, tell me the truth. Do I look fit to meet Marie Rose's in-laws?'

She pirouetted around, displaying her yellow and white floral dress in the traditional Tahitian style. Roland beamed admiringly.

'You look gorgeous,' he replied. 'There's just one thing missing.'

Reaching forward, he plucked a yellow hibiscus bloom from a vase on the table, dried the stem and put the flower in Claire's hair.

'There,' he said. 'Perfect.'

Claire smiled ruefully.

'I don't know about the flower, Papa,' she murmured. 'Marie Rose wants us to look dignified.'

'Dignified!' exclaimed Roland in horror, reaching for the coffee-pot. 'This isn't a family that cares about looking dignified, it's a family that cares about being happy. You can tell Marie Rose I said so. And tell her to get out of bed too or we'll miss the ferry.'

Yet when Roland dropped them off at the waterfront just before nine o'clock, Marie Rose did not go to the ferry office. Instead she led the way along the waterside path that bordered the Boulevard Pomare.

'Where are you going?' demanded Claire. 'The ferry's over that way.'

'I know,' agreed her sister. 'But I've organised a ride on a private launch.'

Claire followed her in silence, intent on watching her steps on the uneven pavement. A listless, salt-laden breeze was blowing in from the harbour and the air was heavy with the scents of diesel oil and tropical flowers. Overhead banks of grey cloud were building ominously, bringing the threat of an impending squall. A few foreign tankers were moored in the harbour and a row of luxury yachts was tied up along the water's edge. As they came towards these, Claire was conscious of a sudden spasm of memory that was almost a physical pain.

'What's wrong?' asked Marie Rose, looking at her pale face and haunted eyes. 'Do you feel sick?'

'No,' replied Claire, gritting her teeth. But a pang had gone through her as she realised that this was the very spot where she had met Marcel Sauvage all those years ago. Marcel has made it impossible for me to feel free and relaxed in my own home, she thought bitterly. Not to mention ruining any chance I had of friendship with Alain Charpentier. Well, thank heaven I don't have to face Alain again for a while anyway!

Which made it all the more of a shock when Marie Rose led her aboard a gleaming white motor launch and babbled an obviously well prepared speech.

'Ah. All ready and waiting for us, I see? I'd like you all to meet my sister Claire Beaumont. Claire, you already know Alain, don't you? And these are my future parents-in-law Denise and Charles Halévy. And their friend Nadine Hugo.'

Claire's swift, horrified gaze met Alain, unsmiling in immaculate white shorts and matching shirt, and she murmured something incoherent. Then the habit of long years in front of TV cameras took over and she turned pleasantly to the other members of the party.

'How do you do?' she said with a warm smile.

Charles Halévy was a grey-haired man with vivid, blue eyes and a humorous expression, while his wife had piercing brown eyes and a pinched mouth. They both returned Claire's greeting civilly enough, although Denise looked her up and down closely like a TV director conducting an audition. But it was the third member of the party, a woman of about thirty, who really caught Claire's attention. Nadine Hugo was small and very well groomed, as if she had just been taken out of a plastic wrapper. Her ginger hair was cut into a geometric style, her tawny eyes were enhanced by a mere suspicion of eyeshadow and she wore a tailored suit of lightweight pale green linen. In spite of the heat, her legs were encased in sheer stockings and white peep-toe shoes which showed off her tiny feet.

'Hello,' she murmured languidly, extending two beautifully manicured fingers to Claire.

'Hello,' said Claire. 'Are you living in Tahiti, Miss Hugo, or just visiting for Paul and Marie Rose's wedding?'

Nadine shuddered.

'Oh, just visiting,' she replied. 'I'm staying for six weeks and that's quite long enough, believe me! Of course, Tahiti's very pretty in a primitive sort of way, but there's nothing to do here, is there?'

'Oh, I don't know,' responded Claire with a twinge of annoyance. 'Over a hundred thousand Tahitians seem to occupy themselves somehow.'

A faint, superior smile hovered round the corners of Nadine's glossy red lips.

'Yes. Well, it's lucky they're easily pleased, isn't it?' she retorted. 'But, as for me, I'll be only too glad to return to Paris and the Montmartre cafés.'

'Montmartre?' echoed Claire. 'Oh, then you really are a close neighbour of the Halévys!'

'And the Charpentiers,' added Nadine. 'In fact, Alain and I often used to share a cab to work when he lived in Paris, didn't we, *chéri*?'

As she spoke, she put one arm around Alain's shoulders and leaned her head playfully against his arm. Her expression was so blatantly seductive that Claire expected Alain either to scowl or burst out laughing. But, to her dismay, he did neither. Instead he stood looking down at Nadine for a moment with a strangely nostalgic look in his dark eyes.

'Ah, yes. Those were the days,' he agreed with an undertone of bitterness. 'Back when life was simple and I hadn't fallen a victim to the lure of the South Seas. Perhaps I would have been wise to stay there.'

'Perhaps you would,' murmured Nadine. 'But it's not too late to change your mind.'

A wave of uneasiness surged through Claire and she turned away, feeling as if she were spying on a private conversation. Did Nadine really have to gaze up at Alain with that breathless fervour, as if she were longing for him to fling her on one of the blue-cushioned lounge seats and ravish her? Even worse, did Alain have to look down at her as if he found the idea rather tempting? I wonder if a cab was all they shared in Paris, thought Claire sourly. Then, bringing her turbulent emotions firmly under control, she turned back to Alain with a cool smile.

'I expect you'd like to get out beyond the reef before the rain starts,' she pointed out. 'Do you want me to cast off for you?'

'There's no need,' growled Alain. 'I can manage without your help.'

His tone was abrupt, as if he hated the thought of owing anything to Claire, even the trivial favour of untying a rope from a bollard. Claire felt her entire body stiffen with resentment and her dark eyes flashed. For an instant she was on the point of turning her back on Alain and simply marching ashore, but Marie Rose was staring at her with a miserable, imploring expression. For an instant the friction between Alain and Claire scorched the air, as potent as the threat of approaching thunder. Then, with an uneasy glance at the two combatants, Charles Halévy stepped between them.

'I'll cast off for you, Alain,' he offered. 'After all, I wouldn't want you to ruin that pretty dress, Miss Beaumont.'

Claire smiled crookedly.

'You're very kind,' she muttered. 'And do please call me Claire.'

Marie Rose gave a faint sigh of relief as the awkward moment passed and Alain sat down at the controls of the launch. Yet Charles was not so easily fobbed off and, when the older man returned, Claire was conscious of his shrewd blue eyes resting thoughtfully on her. However, he said nothing as the engines throbbed into life and Alain turned the craft towards the break in the reef.

'Make yourselves comfortable,' invited Alain, gesturing with one hand towards the luxurious, cushioned lounge seats that lined the walls. 'I'll get you all a drink once we're clear of the harbour.'

For some reason it annoyed Claire unbearably to see how Nadine Hugo immediately chose a seat right next to Alain's swivel chair. Of course, this meant that when Alain turned his chair to look out to starboard his bare, tanned leg brushed against Nadine. Simpering idiot, thought Claire fiercely. Just look at her lapping it up while he apologises for touching her! And any fool can see she'd lie down and strip off every stitch she's wearing if only he'd give the word. Although he's just as bad, with those brooding, sidelong glances he keeps giving her. I don't know where Marie Rose got the idea that he was in love with me, because he certainly doesn't look at me that way. If he did, I wouldn't just sit there with a half-witted grin on my face, I'd...I'd what? For an instant she let herself imagine Alain's smouldering blue eyes searing down over her flesh while his lips curled with that hint of sensual abandonment. She had to admit that the thought was disturbing. Several wildly erotic fantasies flitted before her eyes and an aching throb of desire caught her completely by surprise. She shivered.

'You're not feeling sick, are you?' asked Charles in a concerned voice. 'It does look as though the weather is going to be rather rough out there.'

'No, I'm fine,' protested Claire.

But a glance through the wrap-around windows of the bridge convinced her that Charles was right. Beyond the reef the water was changing from deep blue to murky green and threatening masses of charcoal cloud were piling up above the horizon.

'You don't think it's too dangerous to go, do you, Alain?' asked Nadine uneasily.

Alain shook his head.

'No. It won't be anything worse than a tropical thunder-shower,' he replied. 'Actually it can be quite exhilarating, provided you don't suffer from seasickness.'

Ten minutes later they discovered that he was right as there was a sudden rumble of thunder and the skies opened above them. Rain came hurtling against the windows in violent bursts and the launch thudded into the oncoming seas. Claire, who was an excellent sailor, stood with her legs braced to keep her balance and peered eagerly ahead, enjoying the way the boat moved beneath her like a live thing. But Nadine was not so fortunate. Above the roar of the weather she uttered a plaintive moan and then fled to the tiny bathroom amidships. When she returned, Alain cast her a concerned glance and patted her on the knee.

'Sorry about this,' he said. 'But it'll probably blow itself out by the time we reach Moorea. Why don't you go and lie down in one of the cabins?'

The squall continued thoughout the entire crossing, but suddenly, when they were only a couple of miles from Moorea, it lifted miraculously. Everyone except Alain, who was piloting the launch, and Nadine, who was convinced she was about to die, scrambled out on to the deck to watch the approach of the island. At first it seemed to float like a dark blue cloud between the sea and the sky, as mysterious and beautiful as a mirage. But as they came closer it took on shape and substance. Craggy peaks appeared, a lacy collar of foam marked the contours of the reef and coconut palms waved their fronds like green feather-dusters along the shore line.

'Oh, it's beautiful,' breathed Claire fervently, giving her sister a swift hug. 'You are lucky, Marie Rose, to be marrying somebody you love and living in paradise.'

Marie Rose squeezed Claire's hand.

'I only wish you were doing the same,' she said in a low voice. 'Oh, look! There's Paul down on the wharf. Paul! Paul!'

Marie Rose's fiancé proved to be a large, blond, genial man who came forward to meet them as the launch pulled alongside the wharf. After kissing his parents on both cheeks, he lifted Marie Rose right off her feet, swung her in a whirling circle and deposited her giggling on the concrete. Then he greeted Nadine before turning to Claire.

'It's good to meet you at last,' he said warmly, clasping both her hands in his. 'Marie Rose has told me so much about you. She really misses you a lot, you know.'

'I miss her too,' replied Claire. 'But I'm very happy for you both. I was thrilled when I heard you were getting married.'

'Where would you like your parents' suitcases, Paul?' asked Alain, stepping ashore effortlessly with two heavy bags in his hands and another pair slung around his shoulders.

Paul hurried to help him.

'I've brought the hotel minibus,' he said, gesturing to a smart blue and white vehicle twenty metres away. 'I thought you might all like to do the circle island tour that we'll be giving the hotel guests when they arrive.'

Once aboard the bus, Paul swung himself into the driver's seat and turned with a smile to the others.

'Sit on the left side,' he advised. 'Then you'll get a view of the sea.'

Marie Rose, chattering a mile a minute, plumped herself down in the front passenger seat beside Paul. With so many spare places, the others could easily have occupied a windowseat apiece, but Nadine had other ideas. Sinking gracefully down, she patted the blue padded cushion beside her and smiled up at Alain.

'Do sit beside me, Alain,' she pouted. 'Then you can explain all the sights to me.'

There was very little that needed any explanation, Claire thought impatiently, as the bus pulled away from the wharf. Moorea was an idyllic place where man's imprint was barely visible and the distant roar of the surf on the reef, the glimpses of occasional thatched huts or outrigger canoes drawn up on a white sandy beach would have been more enjoyable without Nadine's incessant babble. But as the bus made its way around the island at a leisurely pace of fifteen miles per hour, the French girl kept up a non-stop interrogation and commentary on everything she saw. 'Alain, what are those spiky bushes growing over there? Pineapples? Is it true that vanilla was once the largest crop on the island? Did you know that the name Moorea means "yellow lizard"? Well, of course, you did, you're an expert on French Polynesia, aren't you? I've heard that all the local people want to do is enjoy themselves fishing and dancing. Is that true? Doesn't it make it difficult to find reliable staff?' And on and on. By the time they had reached Cook Bay, Denise Halévy had dozed off and Claire was ready to scream.

How can Alain bear it? she wondered in disbelief. I know Nadine is glamorous and well dressed and he's known her for aeons, but can't he see how boring she is? To listen to her, you'd think she was an expert on the islands and yet she seems to have missed every single thing that makes them so special. She doesn't even have the sensitivity to be quiet for a while and let the atmosphere of the place flow over her. So what on earth does Alain see in her?

'Oh, look!' cried Nadine, as they rounded a curve in the road.

It was not the magnificent spectacle of the bay that she was pointing to with its sheet of glassy green water and the towering crags on the opposite shore, but a low building with a sign outside.

'The Pearl Centre!' exclaimed Nadine. 'Oh, do stop, Paul! I desperately want to buy some black pearls to take back to Paris.'

At the words 'black pearls' Denise Halévy woke with a start and added her entreaty to Nadine's. With a grin and a shake of his head, Paul stopped the bus and let them all climb out. As Alain stepped to the ground, he turned and offered his hand to Nadine. It might have been only courtesy, but his gaze lingered on the opinionated little redhead far longer than mere courtesy demanded. There was something about that grave, searching expression that stabbed Claire to the heart. Even if he wasn't in love with Nadine, it was clear that he felt a deep wholehearted respect for her—the sort of respect he had never felt for Claire. Which made it all the more distressing when he released Nadine's hand and reached up to help Claire. She did not miss the small, contemptuous tightening of his mouth or the narrowing of his blue eyes as they met hers.

'Thank you,' she said, pulling her hand away as if she had been stung.

Suddenly she knew without a shadow of a doubt that she could not bear to go into the Pearl Centre and watch Nadine flirting with Alain. Nor to watch the way he responded to it. She did not stop to try and analyse why the thought gave her such pain. All she knew was a blind urge to escape. Ducking her head, she strode hurriedly away along the road.

'Claire!' cried Marie Rose in amazement. 'Where are you going? Aren't you coming inside with us?'

'No, thanks,' said Claire in a muffled voice. 'I've got a bit of a headache. I'll walk on towards the hotel and you can catch me up when you're ready.'

I should never have come, she thought desperately as she hurried along the grass verge. I should have known any encounter with Alain Charpentier was bound to be pure disaster for me. If only he didn't have that appalling sexual magnetism about him. I feel such a fool when my mouth goes dry and my heart starts pounding whenever he comes near me. And it's not as if he even likes me. All he's interested in is that superficial, conceited Nadine. Well, I wish something would happen to show him she's not so perfect as he thinks!

Miserably Claire left the roadside and began wandering down a muddy track leading to the bay. She was so preoccupied by her thoughts that she did not even notice the clouds gathering again overhead. Until with a thunderous boom the skies opened and rain poured down in a soaking torrent.

CHAPTER THREE

'OH, NO,' groaned Claire.

Her first intention had been to walk along the path that led around the waterfront to the hotel. But with the driving rain that was now falling this was impossible. Already wet from the previous storm, the path was now beginning to vanish beneath a chain of muddy brown puddles. The only sensible thing Claire could do was run back to the bus and rejoin the others. With a gasp of frustration she swung round and launched herself into the battering downpour. Before she had gone more than ten yards she was drenched to the skin and her hair was flapping in wet streamers about her face. The rain was coming down so heavily that she was half blinded by its force and, stepping unwarily on a loose stone, she tripped and fell headlong in the mud.

'Damn!' she cried angrily.

Stumbling to her feet, she ran on, feeling ready to sob with annoyance. Just her luck! And how infuriating that it had to happen when Nadine Hugo was waiting for her on the bus. She could just imagine the smug way that Nadine would greet her when she returned looking like a survivor from a flash flood. And not only Nadine, but also Alain. No doubt he'd be very amused to see Claire making such a fool of herself!

Yet at that moment Claire blinked and saw a powerful figure sprinting through the rain towards her. She had never seen Alain running before and she could not help feeling a surge of admiration. His powerful, male body was quite simply magnificent. His damp hair clung close to his head and his wet clothes revealed the virile outlines of a physique that was completely primitive in its appeal. He was brandishing a large black oilskin slicker in his hand and, as he drew near, he flung it around Claire's shoulders like a matador swirling a cape. The garment enclosed the pair of them in a makeshift tent, cutting off some of the roar of the storm. Claire's nostrils filled sharply with the distinctive scent of Alain's aftershave and the warm, clean smell of his body.

'W-what are you doing?' she demanded as he adjusted the raincoat so that it covered both of them.

'Trying to save you from looking like a drowned rat,' he replied curtly. 'Although I must say you already do.'

Claire flushed, suddenly conscious of the huge splash of mud all over the front of her dress. Conscious too that her clothes, like Alain's, were clinging to her closely. She saw him glance swiftly at the taut peaks of her nipples under the damp cloth and then look just as swiftly away. Her whole body went rigid with embarrassment and some other indefinable emotion. Twisting away from him, she tried to fling off the oilskin.

'Thank you,' she said stiffly. 'But you shouldn't have bothered.'

'Don't be a fool!' retorted Alain roughly. 'You're my guest and it's my responsibility to look after you. Now get under this jacket at once!'

Claire flinched at the brusqueness of his tone, but obeyed. Alain's muscular arm tensed around her shoulders as he drew her under the shelter, enclosing her tightly, and she could not help being aware of every movement that he made. The sense of intimacy was alarming, but Alain did not even seem to notice it. After a swift, unsmiling glance, he lowered his head and strode forward vigorously, making no concessions to her shorter legs or hampering skirt, so that she had to scurry to keep up.

Claire had a disturbing sense of *déjà vu*, as if this whole incident had happened to her before. And then with vivid certainty she remembered when. It was a long time ago, before Marcel had arrived to wreck her life. One afternoon she had been caught out on Acajou Beach in just such a tropical downpour and Alain had come striding to her rescue with an umbrella. She could see him now, his aloofness banished by the ridiculous intimacy of the occasion. Could see herself too, gauche and tongue-tied, speechless with delight at the twist of fate that had thrown them together. She cringed inwardly at the memory, feeling as if the intervening years had somehow vanished. Trotting along beside Alain, she felt as if nothing had changed and she was still the shy, awkward teenager she had been then. A feeling which was deeply unsettling. Particularly since it was accompanied by the same fluttering awareness of Alain's masculinity that had caused her such torments in the past. Was it really possible that she still had a crush on Alain? she wondered incredulously. Certainly his kiss the previous day had awoken a disturbing physical craving deep inside her. But she was old enough now to know that sexual chemistry didn't necessarily equate with love or even liking. And while Alain obviously felt the same urgent physical attraction towards her, she wasn't fool enough to imagine that he liked her. No, the whole situation was impossible! And, as for Marie Rose's optimistic belief that Alain was in love with her, it was plainly ludicrous. All in all, the sooner Claire could escape from this damned raincoat, the happier she would be!

By the time they reached the roadside, the tropical downpour was easing off as abruptly as it had started. With an expressionless face, Alain whisked the oilskin off Claire's head, folded it briskly and stuffed it under his arm. Then he gave her a faint, hard smile that didn't reach his eyes.

'You should be all right now,' he said. 'Although I doubt if Paul will be thrilled to have you aboard his nice, clean bus.'

He was right. When they rejoined the others, Paul gave a loud guffaw of amusement at Claire's bedraggled appearance.

'You little mud crab!' he exclaimed. 'Stay right there until I get a sheet of plastic for you to sit on.'

Ridiculously, Claire felt her eyes begin to fill with tears. Through the windows of the bus she could see Nadine wearing an expression of haughty amusement and Denise Halévy looking frankly disgusted.

'Don't bother, Paul!' begged Claire miserably. 'I don't want to get your bus all dirty. 'I'll be happy to walk.'

'Then I'll join you,' chipped in Alain unexpectedly.

Claire stared at him in horror, but before she could protest Paul spoke again.

'Don't be ridiculous, both of you,' he said. 'You know I was only teasing, Claire. Hop in and we'll have you back at the hotel in no time.'

Claire hesitated, but at that moment Marie Rose appeared in the doorway of the bus beside her fiancé. There was a speculative gleam in her eye that made her sister feel deeply uneasy.

'Actually it might be better if you and Alain do walk, Claire,' she suggested. 'It isn't far and it will give you a chance to chat about old times.'

Claire felt a pang of dismay and, glancing sideways, she saw Alain's lower lip curl with sardonic amusement. Obviously he could read Marie Rose's motives just as well as she could, but surprisingly he made no objection.

'All right,' he agreed indifferently. 'But can you and Paul lend us some clean clothes when we get there?'

'Sure,' replied Marie Rose. 'We're all going to the restaurant in the main building and I've told the chef we want lunch at one o'clock, so that will give you half an hour to get cleaned up. Just go to our house and borrow whatever clothes you want from our bedroom. There are two bathrooms, so you should be all right. But don't get mud on my new carpets or I'll personally murder you both. OK?'

'OK,' said Claire in a subdued voice.

To her relief, Alain did not talk at all on the remainder of the walk, although he did cast her one or two disturbingly keen glances. They crunched along the damp gravel verge of the road and Claire tried to concentrate on the scents and sights around her. The smell of salt air, the yellow hibiscus dripping with raindrops, the changing play of light and darkness as the clouds fled before the breeze, sending their shadows scurrying across the emerald hills. Anything to take her mind off the man striding beside her, whose brooding presence seemed to reduce her to a quivering heap. It was a relief when they turned into the hotel driveway. Paul and Marie Rose's house proved to be a thatched building in the native style surrounded by a lush garden and with a superb view over the bay. It was so beautiful that Claire was startled into comment.

'Isn't Marie Rose lucky?' she exclaimed, following Alain on to the veranda. 'I'd give my eye-teeth to live somewhere like this.'

'Would you?' asked Alain in an odd voice.

Then he seized the front door handle.

'It's not locked, is it?' asked Claire.

'No. Nobody ever locks anything on Moorea,' replied Alain, turning the handle.

They found themselves in a cool, marble-floored hallway with another corridor leading off at right angles. Claire felt intensely self-conscious about finding herself alone with Alain. Yet his manner was quite impersonal as he advised her to wash her filthy feet in the laundry sink before setting foot on the carpet. And when she lost her balance, standing on one leg, and had to hop around shrieking and flailing desperately, he came to her aid and steadied her. Even so, his manner as he led her to the master bedroom was cool to the point of rudeness.

'I'll shower and change in the other bathroom,' he said curtly, tossing a pair of shorts and a polo shirt on to the bed. 'You can meet me on the veranda when you're ready.'

And, holding the clean clothes at arm's length, he picked his way cautiously out of the door. Left alone, Claire shook her head unhappily, wounded by his obvious hostility. *If only I'd never met Marcel, perhaps Alain and I could have been really good friends,* she told herself. A strange pang went through her at the thought. Perhaps because the image of Marcel still haunted her, although not from any feelings of love towards him. Quite the reverse. The emotions which swept through her whenever she thought of Marcel Sauvage were all negative. Guilt, torment, disgust, rage, despair. Yet by now she had become adept at shutting it all out with a clang like the closing of a fire door. There was no way she could change what had happened, so it was better to ignore it. All the same, she couldn't help feeling an odd, wistful yearning for Alain to like her. Was that still possible or not?

Ten minutes under a warm shower and a leisurely perusal of Marie Rose's wardrobe made Claire feel both cleaner and more hopeful. She chose a pink tie-dyed pareu, sprayed herself liberally with some of Marie Rose's heavenly French perfume and pulled on a pair of leather sandals. As she sat down to fasten the straps, she noticed guiltily that she—or perhaps Alain—had left a steak of brown mud along the caramel-coloured carpet.

'Oh, dear,' she murmured. 'My little sister isn't going to like that at all. I'd better get a sponge or something from the laundry and see if I can clean it up.'

As she padded back along the hall shortly afterwards, she glanced outside, but the veranda was deserted, so she assumed that Alain was still under the shower. Consequently she was completely taken aback when she pushed open the bedroom door and found him standing in front of the chest of drawers with only a knotted towel around his waist.

'Oh!' she gasped, backing away. 'I'm sorry. I thought you were still in the other bathroom.'

'It's my fault,' he said hastily. 'I thought you'd left.'

There was a moment's strained silence and Claire distinctly heard her heart bumping against her ribs. In spite of the towel, she felt agonisingly conscious of Alain's nearness and masculinity. A faint, warm odour that was primitive and deeply erotic emanated from him. It was a scent reminiscent of salt air or wild parsley that filled her with an insane urge to step forward and boldly strip the covering from around his hips. Unconsciously she darted a swift downward glance at him and was tormented by the contours of his flat muscular belly and the line of dark hair that plunged out of sight. She swallowed hastily and looked away, conscious that her cheeks were burning. Alain looked at her with narrowed, watchful eyes.

'W-what are you doing here?' she stammered.

'Paul's shorts didn't fit me so I came back for another pair. The room was empty, so I thought——'

'There was mud on the carpet,' she babbled nervously. 'I went to get a——'

Then suddenly, incredibly, he just swept her into his arms. The embrace was so raw, so violent, so overwhelming that Claire had no time to resist. The sponge dropped unheeded from her fingers as Alain caught her against him. She made a soft, choking sound in the back of her throat, then, without any conscious intention, she kissed him back. The room seemed to spiral around her in a dizzying kaleidoscope of sensations as Alain's warm mouth forced her lips apart. At the touch of his tongue, fire pulsed through her veins. Closing her eyes, she let herself melt sensually into his embrace. His hands were hard and urgent and maddeningly skilful, kneading her back and trickling deliciously down to the base of her

spine. Then with a low groan, he cupped her buttocks
fiercely in his hands and hauled her against him. There
was nothing subtle about the movement and the warm,
quivering thrust of his masculinity against her left her
in no doubt of what he wanted.

Reason told her to call a halt, but reason seemed a
poor substitute for the tide of primitive, urgent longing
that was sweeping through her. Instead of protesting,
she uttered a series of soft, mewing cries, wound her
arms around his neck and kissed him lingeringly. She
could feel the frantic thudding of his heart and his swift,
shuddering intake of breath, then his hard, muscular
thigh forced its way between her legs. Coarse, masculine
hair rubbed against the silky smoothness of her own skin
and all she could feel was an abandoned, wanton delight. Pointing her toe, she drew her own leg up so that
the sole of her foot ran teasingly up the back of his calf.

'You sensual little witch,' he groaned. 'I always knew
you'd be like molten fire, but even in my wildest fantasies I never expected this. Come here, damn you...!'

With a sudden swift movement, he lifted her right off
the floor and stood, gloating down at her. His face was
suffused with passion and his eyes looked dark and
strange. Somewhere, distantly, warning bells rang in
Claire's head. She knew that this encounter was pure
madness, but she was in no mood to listen to warnings,
even her own. The moment Alain had laid his hard,
urgent hands on her, she had been aware of nothing but
a torment of throbbing, sensual need. And, as he strode
purposefully towards the huge, king-size bed, her body
arched towards him in a convulsive spasm of longing.
Then abruptly he flung her down and crouched over her,
his eyes glittering.

'Do you know how badly I want you?' he demanded
hoarsely.

Her breasts were heaving with the shallow, rapid intake
of her breath and she found she could not speak. But

she nodded mutely. He picked up a strand of her long, damp hair and drew it slowly through his teeth.

'You're like a fire in my blood,' he muttered. 'Sometimes I think I'll go out of my mind with wanting you. I thought perhaps you were indifferent to me, but it's the same for you, isn't it? The same frenzy, the same desperate, intoxicating need that takes no account of reason? You want me too, don't you, Claire?'

She shuddered.

'Say it,' he rasped.

Her eyes met his, darted away again.

'Yes,' she whispered.

His hands tightened exultantly in her hair, bunching it in a frame around her face.

'Tell me,' he coaxed in a husky voice that sent tingles of excitement through her. 'Tell me that you want me.'

'I—I want you,' she responded and gave a low gasp as his right hand moved from her hair and slipped sensually down inside her pareu.

'Badly?' he prompted, tracing a whorl of fire on her nipple.

She moaned softly.

'Badly,' she breathed.

His other hand was still resting on her hair and she turned her head suddenly and bit him softly on the warm cushion of flesh at the base of his thumb.

'Oh, would you?' he growled, seizing her jaw in mock reproof. 'You need taming, you little hell cat!'

'Do I?' purred Claire.

And with a sudden, swift movement she drew his thumb into her mouth and sucked on it hard. A thrill of mingled shock and excitement sparked through her as she saw his response to that teasing caress. His entire body stiffened, his eyes flashed fire and, without warning, he lowered himself on to her, crushing her warm curves mercilessly beneath him. Seizing her hands, he

pinioned them above her head and then took her mouth
in a long, sensual kiss that left her aching for more.

'Yes,' said Alain in a hard voice. 'And I'm going to
enjoy taming you, believe me.'

A tide of warmth seemed to be pulsing through her
entire body, urging her to press closer to him and filling
her with impetuous need. However hard she strained
against him, she could not get enough of that powerful,
masculine body whose weight was imprisoning her so
satisfactorily. Yet as Alain's hand suddenly travelled
downwards and began to stroke the inner surface of her
thigh, some vestige of sanity asserted itself.

'We can't,' she said thickly. 'The others——'

'Damn the others!' retorted Alain. 'Marie Rose will
fob them off. You know, your legs are like satin. I'm
going to kiss them all the way up, starting from your
feet.'

His warm, ticklish breath caressed her toes and she
giggled and squirmed, beset by an urge to let him do
whatever he chose with her. He was sensual, playful,
arrogant and she wanted him with a hunger that both
elated and appalled her. Never mind that she had sworn
off men forever, nor that Alain did not love her but was
driven only by lust. It might be simple insanity or a bio-
logical drive as old as time, but, whatever it was, Claire
felt driven by it as relentlessly as a lemming heading for
a cliff. But as Alain's quivering lips brushed the inside
of her thigh, there was an approaching hail from outside
the house.

'Yoohoo! Alain! Claire! Wherever have you got to?'

Alain swore violently and rose to his feet.

'My aunt has the worst sense of timing of any woman
I've ever met,' he said through his teeth. 'Go and tell
her I'm still getting dressed, will you?'

He hauled Claire unceremoniously off the bed and on
to her feet. Then, as he was propelling her towards the

door, he stopped and dragged her against him for another swift, brutal kiss.

'There are things we need to discuss,' he growled. 'I'll pick you up for dinner tomorrow night at eight. All right?'

Claire stared at him, feeling totally shaken. She was not sure what he meant or what he wanted and the abrupt transition from sensual abandonment to business as usual left her apprehensive and confused. Yet there was no time to argue or press for explanations. Not with the front door of the house opening and Denise Halévy's footsteps sounding in the hall.

'All right,' she breathed.

And, fighting down her misgivings, she went to meet Alain's aunt.

A table was already set on the terrace near the swimming-pool and a waiter dressed in colourful Tahitian shorts and shirt was pouring chilled white wine as Claire approached. She was afraid that what had just happened between her and Alain must be written all over her in letters of fire, but nobody paid her any special attention. Apart from a mischievous, enquiring look from Marie Rose, there was little response from the others as she sat down.

'Where's Alain?' demanded Paul, before judiciously swirling a sip of Chablis around his mouth. 'Thanks, that's fine.'

'He'll be here any minute,' replied Claire. 'He couldn't find any clothes to fit him.'

She was thankful that her voice remained steady, but when Alain arrived it took all her self-control to act naturally. The meal was delicious. An entrée of *poisson cru*, the traditional Tahitian dish of raw fish marinated in lime juice and coconut milk, followed by juicy brochettes of beef, a mound of crisp fried potatoes and a tossed green salad with a pudding of waffles and vanilla ice-cream. But Claire might as well have been eating sand for all the pleasure it gave her. Her whole body was tingling with a heightened physical and emotional awareness and she felt morbidly conscious of the undercurrents of tension within the group. Was it her imagination or was Nadine darting her brief, resentful glances from across the table? And were Charles and Denise Halévy both looking from Claire to Alain whenever they thought they were unobserved? And had Nadine knocked over her glass of wine by accident or on purpose so that Alain would have to mop her up? Yet whatever else might be the product of her fevered inventions, Claire could not doubt that the rare, brooding glances she was receiving from Alain were genuine. All in all, it was rather a relief to her when the coffee was finished and the group broke up.

'Well, what would you like to do now?' asked Paul, apparently unaware of any tension among his guests. 'You can lie down for a rest indoors or lounge around by the pool. And later, when the meal has settled, there's snorkelling or water-skiing on the bay if anyone is interested. Or there's a games room and video lounge inside.'

'And, if anyone wants a really thrilling time, Alain can take them on a tour of the new drainage system and deliver his lecture on hotel planning,' put in Marie Rose, her eyes dancing.

'Spare me!' protested Charles in mock horror. 'In any case, my body clock still seems to be on Paris time, so I think I'll go indoors for a little snooze. What about you, my dear?'

Denise shook her head contemptuously.

'The quickest way to get over jet lag is to adopt the local time as soon as possible,' she said with authority. 'And get plenty of bright sunlight. I intend to stay right here on the patio.'

'Nadine?' prompted Paul.

'Actually, I would like a tour of the drainage system and Alain's lecture,' she announced.

There were groans of disbelief from Paul and Marie Rose, and Nadine looked offended.

'You seem to forget that I'm an architect,' she pointed out tartly. 'There's a lot of hidden work that goes into planning a hotel and I appreciate that, even if the rest of you don't. Alain, will you take me?'

'If you like,' said Alain. 'Anybody else coming?'

Claire's feelings were still in turmoil and the last thing she wanted to do was traipse around a set of drainage ditches while Nadine asked penetrating questions about damp courses, so she hastily refused.

'I'll stay here by the pool,' she replied.

Paul had work to do inside the building, so Claire and Marie Rose soon found themselves alone on the patio with his mother. As Alain and Nadine disappeared around the corner of the building, Denise gave a low sigh of satisfaction.

'It's nice to see those two together again,' she remarked, letting herself down into a banana lounger. 'Such a handsome couple. I always thought it was a dreadful pity when they broke off their engagement.'

'Engagement?' echoed Claire in a startled voice.

'Oh, yes, they were engaged years ago before Alain came to Tahiti,' agreed Denise. 'It was a very suitable match and both families were delighted at the thought of it. The Hugos own a huge construction company and, of course, the Halévys and Charpentiers have a chain of hotels right across France. Alain and Nadine could have been a wonderful help to each other in their business dealings.'

Marie Rose blinked. 'You make it sound like a corporate merger!' she protested.

Denise shrugged.

'Oh, my dear, many marriages are, in families that have any assets to consider. Not everyone marries for love as you and Paul are doing.'

The tone in which she said the words 'marries for love' was decidedly lukewarm. Running a shrewd, assessing eye first over Marie Rose and then Claire, Denise Halévy sighed audibly.

'Of course, one hopes that a marriage will work out, whatever the circumstances,' she added. 'But in my view it's very important that a man should never be ashamed of the woman he wants to make his wife. Alain knew that, however rich or famous the circles he moved in, Nadine would always feel at home in them.'

The two girls exchanged expressive glances. Without a word passing between them, Claire knew that her sister was thinking of the rusting bath in their front garden and the peeling paint on their parents' modest home. Denise could hardly have made it clearer that she considered the Beaumonts complete upstarts to be meddling with Alain or Paul.

'So, if Alain and Nadine were so well suited, what went wrong between them?' asked Claire sharply.

For some reason the thought of Alain's being engaged to Nadine sent a pain like a knife piercing through her. It took her a moment's baffled contemplation to realise that the emotion she felt was jealousy. Not that she was in love with Alain. Far from it. She now felt a grim certainty that Alain's sensual caresses meant nothing whatsoever, that he regarded her simply as a challenge like any other attractive woman. It was not the first time she had met a man like that, but the really astonishing thing was the way she had responded to him. After all, wasn't she an expert at taking evasive action when men became too urgent in their pursuit of her? Hadn't she sworn long ago that she would never, ever be fool enough to let herself get hurt so badly again? So why had she let Alain carry her along on such a surge of frenzied passion? And why was she sitting here now, with her heart pumping unsteadily and a lump in her throat, while she waited to hear about his love for another woman? It didn't make sense.

'Oh, it was just a silly tiff really,' replied Denise tranquilly. 'Alain wanted to bring Nadine out here for two years to get the hotel at Point Cupid up and running. He'd always fancied a stint in Tahiti. But she didn't want to come. She said it was a job for some fool who had worked his way up from being a bell-hop, not for a member of the Charpentier family, and Alain took offence. He came without her and, before we knew it, the engagement was over. But they've never lost touch with each other and it's obvious that there's some very powerful chemistry between them.'

'How can you be so sure?' demanded Marie Rose, darting a troubled look at Claire.

Denise smiled superciliously.

'Oh, my dear, one only has to look at them,' she said. 'Besides, Alain would hardly be sleeping with her, if he felt no attraction at all, would he?'

'Sleeping with her?' whispered Claire in horror.

Denise looked amused.

'Oh, yes,' she said. 'They're going to Bora Bora together for a week or two after Paul's wedding. And I wouldn't think they've booked a double room just to watch television, would you?'

A medley of conflicting emotions surged through Claire's breast. Shock, anger, disbelief, humiliation. Rising to her feet, she paced across to the edge of the patio to hide her confusion from the others. How dared Alain make love to her when he was still sleeping with Nadine? How dared he invite her to dinner and tell her they had things to discuss? The only subject they had to discuss was how Claire could make sure she never saw him again! Her eyes smarted with angry tears.

'Is there any more coffee, Marie Rose?' she asked in a muffled voice.

'Yes, come inside with me and I'll get it,' said Marie Rose, laying an arm protectively around her sister's shoulders. 'You'll excuse us for a moment, won't you, Denise? By the way, can I get you more coffee too?'

'No, I'm perfectly content, thank you,' replied Denise with a small, feline smile.

'I'll bet she is, the old witch!' exclaimed Marie Rose, once they were out of earshot. 'I've never seen such a mischief-maker! Come into Paul's office and tell me what's wrong, Claire.'

A moment later the door closed behind them and they found themselves alone in a pleasant room overlooking the garden.

'Now,' said Marie Rose, settling herself expectantly in an easy-chair and switching on an electric coffee percolator. 'What's the matter, Claire? Is it only because of Denise telling you that Alain is sleeping with Nadine?'

'Only!' said Claire with feeling.

'So he does mean something to you,' suggested Marie Rose softly.

'No!' retorted Claire. 'He doesn't! He doesn't mean a damned thing to me. It's just that——'

'He kissed you while you were over at my house?'

'Kissed!' exclaimed Claire with a strangled laugh. 'I suppose you could call it that.'

Suddenly she hid her face in her hands.

'I should never have come home!' she cried. 'All Alain wants to do is humiliate me. I'm sure that's the only reason he did it.'

'Did what?' asked Marie Rose, gently prising her fingers apart.

'Don't ask!' said Claire savagely. 'I'm sure you can guess. But it doesn't have any meaning for him, Marie Rose. He hates me!'

Marie Rose clicked her tongue sceptically.

'That's not true,' she insisted. 'I've seen the way he looks at you, when he thinks nobody is watching him. There's anger in it, I won't deny it, but there's also a kind of desperate yearning. He really cares about you deeply, Claire, whatever you think.'

'I'm sure,' sneered Claire. 'So deeply that he's sleeping with Nadine Hugo at the same time as he's making up to me!'

'You don't know that for a fact,' pointed out Marie Rose. 'It's only gossip, and probably spiteful gossip into the bargain.'

Claire shrugged expressively.

'Well, it's nothing to me,' she said stonily. 'He can do what he likes with Nadine, for all I care!'

'Can he?' murmured Marie Rose. 'Oh, Claire, you don't have to pretend to me! I'm on your side and I think you ought to try and work out why Alain disturbs you so much. Just think about it for a minute. What exactly do you feel towards him?'

'I loathe him!' blazed Claire. 'I don't trust him further than I could throw him.'

'But you still go weak at the knees with desire when you look at him, don't you?' said Marie Rose.

'I suppose so,' muttered Claire. 'But what of it?'

Marie Rose sighed.

'Doesn't it occur to you that maybe he feels the same way towards you?' she asked. 'That he hates you and loves you equally. And that he feels confused and angry about the way you affect him?'

Claire looked at her with unwilling interest.

'Maybe,' she conceded.

'Then why don't you give each other a chance?' begged Marie Rose. 'Get to know him, Claire.'

'I don't want to get to know him!' retorted Claire. 'He makes me feel unsafe, as if I'm walking on the rim of a volcano. As if I have no power over my life or my emotions. And I hate it. I'm not going to have dinner with him tomorrow night, whatever he says.'

'Is that what he wants you to do?' asked Marie Rose.

'Yes, but I won't,' insisted Claire.

'Do it,' urged Marie Rose. 'Go on, do it. You'll never enjoy anything in life if you go on shutting yourself off, just because of some meaningless quarrel you and Alain had years ago. If you want happiness, you have to be prepared to take risks, Claire!'

'Well, I'm not going to,' said Claire through her teeth. 'As soon as I see Alain again, I'm telling him that the dinner is off!'

But that proved to be more easily said than done. All afternoon Alain had Nadine at his side and Claire had no opportunity to speak to him in private. Even when they returned from Moorea to Tahiti, the French girl stuck to him like a limpet. It was true that when Alain drove the Beaumonts home shortly after nightfall Marie Rose slipped discreetly inside and let Claire alone on the veranda with Alain. Yet she was agonisingly conscious of Nadine, sitting in the car at the end of the driveway. All the same, she did make an effort to speak.

'Alain?' she said unsteadily.

'Yes?'

Moonlight silvered his stern features and the scent of frangipani wafted strongly from an unseen plant in the darkness.

'About this dinner tomorrow night,' she faltered. 'I really don't think I can go. Nadine——'

'Nadine has nothing to do with it,' he cut in. 'And you and I have things to discuss. I'll pick you up at eight o'clock.'

CHAPTER FOUR

WITHOUT another word he turned abruptly and left. Stumbling distractedly into the house, Claire felt dazed to see her mother sitting in the living-room sewing as if nothing had happened. Pushing her glasses up on her hair, Eve set down the sheet she was darning and smiled.

'You must be as restless a sleeper as ever, Claire,' she exclaimed, shaking her head. 'Just look at this sheet! Anyone would think you had had a tug of war with it.'

Claire's worry and confusion gave way to a spurt of amusement, which only increased when Marie Rose flashed her a sly wink. Fortunately their mother was not looking. Pushing aside her sewing gear, she rose to her feet.

'There was a phone call for you while you were out, Claire,' she continued, wandering over to a littered desk. 'It was that nice young cameraman we met in Sydney last year. What's his name? Danny Abbott, is that it? Apparently he's having a week's stop-over in Tahiti on his way to Los Angeles and he wants you to phone him at his hotel. Now, if I can just find my glasses, I'll tell you the phone number.'

'They're on top of your head, Maman,' said Claire, twinkling. Her mother's vagueness was legendary. 'Don't worry, just give me the note and I'll phone him.'

Danny's arrival came as a welcome distraction after the drama of her day with Alain. He was one of the cameramen from *Towards The Future* and, after three years of working together, he and Claire had an easy, bantering friendship.

'It'll be nice to talk to him,' she said, thinking aloud.

'Well invite him over to dinner one night, dear,' urged her mother. 'But not tomorrow, because Papa and I are going to your Aunt Laurette's. And not Saturday, because that's Marie Rose's wedding. It is this Saturday, isn't it, my lamb?'

'Yes, Maman,' agreed Marie Rose with a long-suffering look.

Claire choked down a giggle and fled. Both her parents were absolute darlings, but it sometimes amazed her that either of them ever managed to pay a bill or cross a street unaided. In the kitchen, she picked up the phone and dialled Danny's number.

'Danny? Claire here.'

Danny's cheerful tones boomed down the line.

'G'day, mate,' he exclaimed. 'Guess what? I'm stranded in Tahiti for a week, kicking my heels until the producer gets a story lined up for me in Silicon Valley. Not that I'm complaining, mind you. The weather's terrific and there's plenty of good-looking birds to watch. But what I really need is a quiet candlelit dinner with the girl who's watched by millions in glorious Technicolor every week, the one and only Claire Beaumont. What do you say, love?'

Claire chuckled.

'Danny, have you been drinking?' she demanded.

'I hope you recognise a hurt silence when you hear one,' replied Danny in injured tones. 'No, I haven't been drinking. Or no more than a quick snort anyway. But I do fancy a night on the town tomorrow, so how about joining me for dinner?'

Claire thought guiltily of Alain and hesitated.

'I don't know,' she began.

'Aw, come on,' wheedled Danny. 'You know how hopeless my French is, don't you? For some reason, the only words I can ever remember are "citron" and the numbers from one to six. I'll probably wind up eating half a dozen lemons for dinner if you don't take pity on me!'

Claire gave in.

'All right,' she agreed. 'Where do you want to eat?'

'There's some place in the tourist brochures called the Belle Vista that sounds good. I'll get a hire car and pick you up at seven-thirty and we'll go there. OK?'

'OK,' agreed Claire, with a faint sense of misgiving.

After Danny had rung off, she said goodnight to the others and went to her room. Marie Rose and her mother were comfortably settled at the kitchen table, poring over a seating plan for the wedding, and her father was outside, strumming his ukulele and watching the moon rise over the dark lagoon. It was the sort of evening which had once filled her with deep contentment. All the family at home, pursuing their own separate interests, but enjoying the sense of each other's closeness. But for once it gave Claire no pleasure at all. Instead, a confused feeling of sadness welled up inside her. Not only because Marie Rose was getting married and the family was splitting up forever. It was more than that, worse than that.

Claire felt lonely, miserable, an outsider. Her parents had each other, Marie Rose had Paul, but whom did she have? Nobody. For six years she had pretended that she loved being independent, mobile, completely without ties. But deep down she knew it wasn't true. Somewhere inside her was an aching longing for commitment, permanence, love. And in some incomprehensible way, when she thought of those things now, the image of Alain Charpentier rose before her. So was Marie Rose right? Did Alain love her? And, more frightening still, did the powerful, confused feelings he awoke in her mean that she loved him? But why would he be involved with Nadine Hugo, if all that were true? A low cry of impatience escaped Claire and she paced across to the window and pressed her face against the cool glass.

'I can't possibly stay on here,' she whispered to the silver sea and the dark silhouettes of the coconut palms. 'It's no use. I'll have to go back to Sydney as soon as the wedding is over.'

Yet, surprisingly, she woke the following morning with a feeling of renewed optimism. The sun was pouring down from a vivid blue sky, the sound of children's laughter came from the beach and a breeze was blowing in from the ocean, warm and mild and tinged with salt. It was impossible to feel gloomy on such a day. After a lazy breakfast of crusty French bread and fresh pineapple, Claire came to a decision. As a matter of courtesy, she would have to phone Alain and cancel the dinner. But she had a shrewd suspicion that he would argue with her, so she didn't intend to give him the chance. Instead she would leave it until the last possible moment to contact him.

One of her cousins good-naturedly took her out in his pirogue and she spent a magical day on the turquoise lagoon, snorkelling and catching fish from the brightly painted canoe. When they returned at sunset, she took a quick shower and then phoned Alain's hotel.

'Hello,' she said rather breathlessly. 'This is Claire Beaumont. May I speak to Monsieur Charpentier's secretary, please? No, I don't want to speak to Monsieur Charpentier himself, I just want to leave a message. Can you please tell him that I can't have dinner with him tonight? Tell him ... tell him I have a headache. Thank you.'

'Alain's going to murder you for this,' predicted Marie Rose, filing her nails and shamelessly listening in. 'He's not the kind of man that can be stood up and take it lying down, you know.'

'Well, he'd be a contortionist if he were!' retorted Claire smartly. 'Now for heaven's sake leave me alone,

Marie Rose. Danny will be here soon and I have to get ready. I want to have a really great time tonight.'

Yet for some reason the great time didn't materialise. Danny arrived at seven-thirty looking so reassuringly familiar with his russet beard and twinkling hazel eyes that Claire hugged him. But once they were at the Bella Vista restaurant, she found it impossible to concentrate on what he was saying. The food was good, the band was playing lively foxtrots and Danny was telling her about his idea for a TV programme about a new type of electric car, but her mind kept wandering. Had Alain received her message? Or had he come to her house and found the place in darkness? And, if he had received her message, had he taken Nadine out to dinner instead of her?

'Don't you agree, Claire?' asked Danny.

'Mmm? What? Oh, yes, of course I do!'

Danny looked at her severely.

'Considering I just asked you if an electric car could be fuelled by recycled bubble gum, I'm not sure that your opinion is worth much,' he said. 'Come on, mate, what's the matter? You've been daydreaming all evening.'

Claire smiled wanly.

'I-I'm sorry, Danny,' she stammered. 'I guess I'm just not with it tonight. Would you mind if I went home.?'

Danny's big hand covered hers.

'Whatever you say,' he agreed.

Half an hour later, the hire car turned into the Beaumonts' driveway. Danny opened the door and walked Claire up the path with one arm affectionately round her shoulders.

'Something's wrong, isn't it?' he insisted, bringing her to a halt under the veranda light and gazing seriously at her. 'Can't you tell me what it is?'

'I'm thinking of leaving the TV show and staying here in Tahiti,' blurted out Claire in a rush.

Danny looked taken aback, then he smiled knowingly.

'I get it,' he murmured. 'You've fallen in love with someone, haven't you?'

'No! Yes...I don't know... Maybe,' replied Claire incoherently. 'But I don't know if he even likes me and we keep quarrelling... Oh, Danny, what do you think I should do?'

'Just do what your heart tells you and good luck,' advised Danny. Then he put his arms around her and hugged her. 'I'm pleased for you, mate, and I'm sure it will all work out.'

She clung to him gratefully and stood on her toes to plant a warm kiss on his bearded cheek.

'Thanks, Danny,' she said. 'You really are an awfully nice man.'

'Yeah, I know,' agreed Danny modestly. 'Well, stay in touch, love.'

He flicked her under the chin and was gone. She stayed for a moment on the veranda, biting her lip as she watched the red tail-lights of the car vanish, then she turned the knob on the front door. It opened easily under her hand. Marie Rose must be at home, she thought, dropping her bag on the hall stand. But it was not Marie Rose who turned to face her as she entered the sitting-room. It was Alain.

'You!' she breathed.

His blue eyes glittered dangerously as he took in every detail of her shimmering red flounce-necked dress, the string of pearls around her throat and careful make-up.

'How's your headache?' he asked with a sardonic lift of his black eyebrows.

She flinched.

'What are you doing here?' she demanded. 'How did you get in?'

He gestured towards a couple of cartons lying on the floor.

'More of Aunt Yvette's china,' he replied indifferently. 'The neighbours had a key and let me in. I was just about to leave when you and your... companion arrived.'

'Don't say "companion" in that hateful, sneering way!' protested Claire. 'Danny's an old friend.'

'Oh, I dare say,' purred Alain. 'And I suppose you always kiss your old friends goodbye with such abandon, do you?'

'How do you know I was kissing him?' demanded Claire furiously. 'Were you spying on me?'

'No, I was not spying on you!' grated Alain. 'I couldn't help but notice you through the window from where I was standing. See for yourself.'

It was true. A direct line of sight went from Alain's position to the veranda outside.

'Well, you're twisting everything,' cried Claire, turning back from the window to face him. 'I only kissed Danny because I'm fond of him. There was nothing wrong with what I was doing!'

'Really?' marvelled Alain, and his blue eyes were like opals lit with cold fire. 'You don't think it's the slightest bit rude to break a date with one man so that you can go out with another?'

She shrank, realising that the criticism was unanswerable.

'I'm sorry,' she said huskily.

'Oh, it's not important,' retorted Alain, still raking her body with that fierce, brooding gaze. 'I suppose I should be grateful that you've disillusioned me so expertly. You know, it's a funny thing, Claire. Yesterday I was beginning to wonder whether I was wrong about you, but now I see that I was right all along.'

'What do you mean?' breathed Claire.

He took a step towards her. Then his forefinger touched her forehead and moved slowly, almost lovingly down her cheek until he cupped her chin in his hand. She stood still, scarcely breathing, but aware that she was trembling under his touch.

'What do I mean?' he asked. 'Oh, simply that you really are exactly the way I thought you were. Heartless, deceitful and a compulsive seductress. Well, I'm sorry, sweetheart, but I've no wish to be added to your list of conquests. So I'll see you at the wedding and, after that, I hope to God I never see you again!'

'Wait!' cried Claire, as he made for the door.

He turned back, but his face was so full of antagonism that she hardly knew where to begin. A maelstrom of feelings seethed inside her. Confusion, resentment, yearning, hurt pride. And yet she could not put any of them into words, because she felt as if an abyss were opening up between them. Staring blindly down at the floor with her breast heaving and her eyes stinging with tears, she noted dimly that there was a huge bouquet of red roses sitting on one of the cartons.

'What about the flowers?' she choked. 'Are they for Marie Rose too?'

'No,' said Alain abruptly. 'I brought them for you.'

And he was gone.

Claire did not see him again until the day of Marie Rose's wedding. By then she had brought her turbulent feelings under control, by the simple expedient of ignoring them. And she was determined that Marie Rose's big day should not be spoilt by any prima donna tantrums on her part. All the same, she could not suppress a stab of pure misery when she first saw Alain at the Town Hall.

Like all French weddings, this one had to be celebrated at a civil ceremony before the optional church service, but there was an air of pomp even about this part of the proceedings. The building itself was an imposing replica of an earlier royal palace, painted pink, with white balustrades and a clock tower on the roof. And Marie Rose was firm in her insistence that she wanted every moment captured forever on video. Consequently, when Claire arrived, she had to endure seeing Alain come forward, open the car door and help her out, while both of them smiled hypocritically at the camera. Alain looked remarkably handsome in a morning coat and striped trousers with a red carnation in his buttonhole and his even white teeth gleaming, but Claire was not deceived. She saw the signs of tension in his narrowed eyes and the pulse that beat visibly at his temple. It was a relief when the rest of the wedding party arrived and they all went inside.

When the civil ceremony was over, they climbed into the waiting cars and drove to a pastel-pink church which stood tranquilly overlooking the harbour. But, as they were milling around in front of the pink building with its white gingerbread trim, misfortune struck.

'Oh, no!' exclaimed Claire's cousin Pierre, who was operating the video camera. 'The stupid battery's gone dead.'

'Don't you have a spare?' asked Claire.

He felt in his pocket, grimaced and shook his head. Marie Rose looked ready to burst into tears, but Claire was quick to suggest a solution.

'Danny!' she cried. 'Danny's staying in a hotel just along the waterfront. I'm sure he'd bring his video equipment and help us out.'

A quick phone to call to the pastor's house settled the matter. After a ten-minute delay Danny arrived, festooned with equipment, and the service began. To Claire it was a deeply moving experience, part enchantment and part ordeal. She knew that she would carry thoughts of this day with her for the rest of her life. The thrilling tones of the organ, the sunlight that burnished Marie Rose's white-clad figure, the beaming pride in Paul's face as he watched his bride's approach were all memories that she would cherish forever. And yet there were also darker images and more painful emotions to deal with.

She could not suppress a pang of envy that her little sister was grown up and marrying when she herself had found happiness so elusive. Nor could she turn aside the stab of pure pain that pierced her as Alain moved forward with the ring. Claire herself was just stepping back with Marie Rose's bouquet and their eyes met. The entire church and all its occupants seemed to spin away into oblivion and there was nothing but herself and Alain. She was dimly conscious of the scent of flowers, the golden, filtered light, the hushed, expectant silence of the onlookers as the ceremony reached its climax. With a suffocating sense of panic and excitement, she wondered how it would feel if she and Alain were the ones exchanging vows. Memories of their fiery encounter on Moorea came flooding back to her and for an instant she longed passionately to end their feud. Then she saw the smouldering dislike in Alain's eyes, the faint, contemptuous curl of his lip as he returned her gaze and she yearned for nothing but the chance to escape from him.

It was a long time coming. First there was the fuss of signing the register and then the chaotic milling about on the church steps for photos. A family group with the Beaumont and Halévy parents. The bride and groom in a dozen different poses. Then Marie Rose, Paul, Alain and Claire from several angles. And then worst of all, a portrait of Alain and Claire alone together. Even on her wedding day, it seemed that Marie Rose couldn't resist matchmaking for others.

'Now I'd like some shots of the best man and the bridesmaid,' she told the photographer. 'Nice, informal ones, with their arms around each other. And smiling.'

I'll murder you, little sister, thought Claire furiously. I'll jolly well murder you. Yet she had no choice but to let herself to be pushed into position and to smile radiantly up at Alain. The warmth of his hard, muscular arm seemed to scorch through her coral chiffon dress and she was aware that his smile was as forced and unnatural as her own. But they held their poses obediently until Marie Rose relented.

'All right, that'll do,' she said pertly. 'Now let's go to the reception and have some fun!'

The reception was being held at Alain's hotel on the cliff near Point Cupid and here, at last, Claire was able to melt thankfully into the crowd. While the bride and groom and their parents stood in a reception line shaking hands, Claire plunged into the thick of the arriving guests and tried to make herself useful. She chatted to guests from France, helped an old and rather feeble great-aunt to refreshments, thwarted a couple of enterprising little boys who were sneaking champagne from the buffet and reunited a crying child with her mother. Now and then she caught a glimpse of Alain threading his way through the crowd and realised that he was performing similar errands of mercy. But it was only when the party was in full swing and Claire herself felt justified in sitting down that she encountered him directly. And then only for a moment.

Sinking into a luxuriously cushioned cane chair behind some potted plants, she took a sip of champagne with a grateful sigh and then picked up a cheese and bacon savoury. But as she bit into the delicious flaky pastry, a stray remark from the other side of the pot plants caught her attention.

'I don't understand why Alain's sister Louise didn't come to the wedding. She and Paul were so close as children; it seems rather odd. Do you know why——?'

Claire froze. Up until that moment she hadn't given a thought to Louise's absence, but now a hideous suspicion rose in her mind about why Alain's sister hadn't wanted to come. Could Alain possibly have told Louise how he had found Claire with her husband? If he did, she certainly wouldn't want to confront me face to face, thought Claire miserably, and who could blame her? She was still sitting with her half-eaten savoury forgotten on her plate when she became aware that Alain was staring down at her.

'Oh, Alain!' exclaimed the imperious voice from behind the plants. 'There you are! Tell me, why didn't dear Louise come to the wedding?'

Alain's blue eyes met Claire's in a brief, hostile encounter, then he looked away.

'I really don't know, I'm sorry,' he replied. 'She was certainly sent an invitation, but she wrote back and said she wasn't feeling fit to travel.'

The way his dark eyebrows drew together made Claire wonder agonisingly if he shared her view of Louise's motives. Yet however much he might scowl, at least he had the decency not to voice his suspicions aloud.

'I'm sure she'll be sorry to have missed the wedding,' he said evenly. 'But next time I speak to her, I'll give her your regards, shall I, Great-Aunt Catherine?'

'Yes, yes, dear boy. And, by the way, I hope you can join the rest of us for a family dinner at the Belvedere on Monday evening. I want to hear all about your life here in Tahiti.'

Alain shrugged charmingly.

'I'm afraid I can't accept,' he replied. 'I've arranged to go to Bora Bora with Nadine Hugo on Monday morning.'

Claire felt a cold chill strike through her. So it wasn't any fantasy on the part of Denise Halévy! Alain and the French girl really were going to one of the outer islands together. Suddenly, feeling unable to listen to another word, she rose to her feet. She hadn't intended to eavesdrop, but with such a crowd in the room, it had been impossible to do anything else. Now she was conscious only of an urgent need to escape.

As she stumbled across the room, she bumped straight into Danny. He looked down at her with concern.

'You're awfully pale, mate. Everything all right?'

Tears blurred her eyes and she snatched an agonised glance over her shoulder at Alain before looking up at the brawny cameraman.

'It's just the heat,' she said with a catch in her voice. 'I'll slip outside for some fresh air.'

Danny's hazel eyes took on a murderous glint as his gaze followed hers to where Alain stood. Putting one arm protectively round her shoulders, he gave her a gentle push towards the door.

'Go on then, love,' he whispered in her ear. 'And if that bastard tries to follow you, I'll thump him.'

Threading her way through the densely packed guests, Claire slipped out of the reception room on to a spacious patio surrounding a pool. Even here, there were waiters with trays of golden, bubbling champagne held high above their heads, the hum of lively conversation, bursts of sudden laughter. Slipping between the groups of chattering people, she turned a corner, skipped hastily down some stairs and found herself on a secluded deck overlooking the lagoon. She took a couple of deep breaths, trying to regain her composure. Yet even here she was not alone. A thickset man seated on a garden chair, glanced up guiltily at her approach. Claire gave a low gasp of surprise.

'Papa! Whatever are you doing here?' she asked.

'Just having a little rest,' he muttered. 'I sneaked away.'

As she came closer she saw with concern that his lips were blue and that he panted slightly as he spoke.

'Are you all right?' she asked in dismay. 'Shall I fetch a doctor? Or Maman?'

She was already moving backwards, ready to fetch help, but he seized her wrist and shook his head.

'No, *chérie*,' he begged. 'It's nothing new, this breathlessness, and I've taken my tablets. All I need to do now is give them a chance to work. And I don't want to go upsetting Marie Rose on her big day. You just let me sit here for a while and I'll be fine again.'

'All right,' agreed Claire unhappily. 'But I'm going to stay and make sure that you are.'

She sat down on another chair beside him and he kept hold of her hand, as he laboured for breath. After a while, she was relieved to see some colour creep back into his grey face. Then he gave her a familiar, conspiratorial wink.

'Well, who'd have thought it?' he mused, gesturing up the stairs. 'Little Marie Rose married, eh? Odd, you know. I always thought you'd be the first, being two years older and the pretty one.'

'Don't, Papa!' begged Claire. 'I've got my career, you know.'

Her father stared at her searchingly.

'But are you sure that's enough for you?' he asked in a troubled voice. 'I don't know, Claire, I'm not an educated man and I never made a real success of any job I had. But I do know this. You two girls and your mother have always meant everything in the world to me, far more than any career ever could have done. And I don't like to think of you missing out on that kind of happiness.'

Claire forced a smile.

'Oh, I'm not missing out on anything, Papa!' she assured him. 'I'm perfectly happy with my job. I always have been.'

Roland sighed.

'Well, if you say so,' he agreed dubiously. 'And you know I'm proud of you, *chérie*. But if I'd known what was going to happen when you went off to Australia, I'm not sure that I'd have let you go. I only wanted you to see a bit of the world and stretch your wings for a year or so. I never dreamt you'd stay there permanently.'

'I'm sorry,' murmured Claire inadequately.

'Don't be,' urged Roland. 'It's your life. But I can't help feeling sad that you didn't settle here in Tahiti. The place just doesn't seem the same without you.'

Claire was touched by the pathos of these words, delivered with such simplicity. Putting one arm around her

father's shoulders, she stared out at the blue vista of the
ocean beneath them and bit her lip. Her throat tightened
as she thought of leaving her family yet again. But as
long as Alain Charpentier continued to hate her, there
was no way she could remain in Tahiti. Whatever she
felt for him, whether love or some strange alchemy of
the emotions, she could not bear to stay here and know
that he detested her.

'Come on,' she said brightly, jumping to her feet and
offering her hand to Roland. 'They'll be cutting the cake
soon and it would never do for us to miss that.'

They arrived back in the reception room just as the
waiters were setting up the three-tiered white wedding
cake on the central table. Marie Rose and Paul stood
beaming joyfully in their wedding finery while cameras
flashed and female relatives dabbed their eyes. Then the
toasts began. It was the usual routine for any wedding,
but Claire found her heart beating faster when Paul pro-
posed a toast to the bridesmaid and Alain replied on her
behalf. She had half feared that he would make some
sardonic remark, but Alain was nothing, if not correct.
His compliments about her beauty and talent would have
touched her profoundly, if only he had looked at her as
he spoke. Instead, he stared at a spot just beyond her
left shoulder, effectively avoiding all contact with her.
She was glad when she looked at the clock on the wall
and saw that it was time for Marie Rose to go and change.
At least the ordeal would be over soon.

'Come on,' she urged, gripping her sister by the elbow.
'You and Paul will miss your flight to Europe if you
don't leave soon.'

Ten minutes later, Marie rose appeared dressed in a
chic apple-green suit and everyone crowded out on to
the hotel steps to bid a last farewell to the newlyweds.

'Wait, wait,' cried Marie Rose, as Paul tried to coax
her away from embracing relatives and into the waiting
car. 'There's one more thing I have to do!'

She brandished her wedding bouquet and smiled mischievously.

'I know it's not the custom in Tahiti,' she said. 'But in Australia, where my mother grew up, brides throw their bouquet to the unmarried women and whoever catches it will be the next one to marry. So, line up, girls!'

There were squeals of excitement as all the unmarried females from eight to seventy-two took their places.

'Ready?' cried Marie Rose.

Then, with unashamed favouritism, she flung the bouquet high over the heads of everyone else and into her sister's hands. Claire let out a groan of laughter.

'Don't be silly!' she protested, but there were whistles and cheers from the other guests.

'You'll be next,' said one of her cousins teasingly.

'No, I won't!' vowed Claire. 'I don't intend to marry, so I'm afraid it will be a case of "Always a bridesmaid, never a bride"!'

'Just as well,' muttered Alain under his breath.

Claire heard the remark and half turned to face him. She felt as shocked and dismayed as if he had struck her. Suddenly, amid all that laughing, milling crowd, it was as if they were alone.

'Why do you say that?' she challenged, hating herself for rising to the bait, but unable to resist.

'Because I can't imagine you ever being content with one man,' was the cruel reply.

Claire felt her cheeks grow hot with anger and humiliation. But at that moment there was a sudden uproarious cheer, as the car, weighted down with boots and old tin cans, pulled out of the driveway. She waved and shouted along with everyone else and felt herself grow a little calmer. Well, at least nobody heard Alain say that, she told herself. Nobody else realises how much he dislikes me. But she was wrong. When she turned back towards the hotel foyer she saw her father gazing from her to Alain with a look of anxious bewilderment on his face.

'What's wrong between you two?' he asked, as they went back into the hotel. 'Why was Alain so rude to you?'

'It's nothing. Nothing, Papa,' she said in a strained voice. 'Please don't give it a moment's thought.'

Yet she could see her father's uneasiness as they stood farewelling the other guests and, when it was time for the Beaumonts themselves to leave, she made a valiant effort to reassure him. Alain came to the front door of the hotel to see them into their car and Claire did something which surprised him very much. After her parents had said goodbye and climbed into the car, she stood on tiptoe and kissed Alain warmly on both cheeks. He looked startled.

'Thank you for everything,' said Claire, enunciating crisply. 'You've really helped to give Marie Rose an unforgettable wedding. But I want you to know how much I've enjoyed the time I've spent with you too. You've been wonderful.'

Alain's eyes narrowed suspiciously. He gripped her arms and his fingers dug into her flesh.

'You're lying,' he breathed. 'Why?'

Claire darted a swift, anxious glance at her father, cocooned behind the windows of the car, but watching her and Alain with interest. Turning away so that Roland could not read her lips, she spat out her response.

'All right, I'm lying,' she hissed. 'But I'm prepared to lie in a good cause. My father heard what you said to me and it upset him. He's not well and I don't want him to worry, so, if you've any compassion at all, for heaven's sake play along with me.'

Without a moment's hesitation, Alain swept her into a crushing hug.

'I've missed you so badly while you were away,' he said hoarsely. 'But it's been wonderful to see you again. I'm only sorry that you have to leave so soon.'

Claire felt a heart-stopping moment of pure joy as his arms tightened around her. Then she reminded herself fiercely that this was only acting.

'Yes, well,' she replied briskly. 'It's been lovely to see you too, Alain, but I've got my job to get back to. Still, if I come again next year, maybe we can get together.'

Alain had his back to the car, so it did not matter that his eyes became suddenly hostile.

'Maybe we can,' he agreed indifferently. 'But I'll say goodbye now. I'm off to Bora Bora on Monday, so I don't suppose we'll see each other again.'

Claire swallowed the lump in her throat.

'No, I don't suppose we will,' she said.

He seemed on the point of saying something else, but then he evidently changed his mind. Clamping his lips together, he turned and wrenched open the car door.

'Get in,' he ordered.

And, without another word, he slammed the door and walked away. Claire was still gazing after him when another figure appeared beside the car.

'Danny!' she exclaimed, winding down the window.

'You look a bit down in the mouth, love,' said the good-natured Australian. 'Weddings do that to people, don't they? So listen, what do you say to going out on the town with me for a few hours?'

Claire shot a quick glance at the hotel entrance, where Alain was standing with his arms folded and a grim expression on his face. Yet she could have sworn he was listening. A defiant rush of adrenalin surged through her. Well, she'd show him a thing or two!

'Good idea, sweetheart,' she replied clearly. And for good measure she gave the startled Danny a provocative kiss on the lips. 'Pick me up in half an hour.'

* * *

In a curious way the evening with Danny helped to soothe Claire's troubled feelings. Not that it was in any way the sizzling orgy which she hoped Alain was imagining. After so many years of working with Danny, Claire felt she could trust him like a brother. And, like a brother, he joked and teased and coaxed her out of her misery. Danny's view of the situation was extremely simple. If Alain was going to treat Claire decently, she should stay and marry him. If not, Danny would personally disembowel him and then put Claire on a plane for Sydney. This barbarous solution to her problems made Claire choke with laughter and Danny quickly followed up his advantage by persuading her to dance. After several hours amid the raucous vitality of the La Cave nightclub her spirits were restored. But it's like taking aspirin for an aching tooth, she thought as they drove back to Acajou Beach at two o'clock in the morning. It doesn't really change anything, it only numbs the pain for a while.

Yet as they turned into her parents' yard, the pain flared up again with agonising insistence. Alain's Citroën was parked in the driveway and there were lights on in the house.

'I hope nothing's wrong,' said Claire on a sharp, rising intonation. 'That's Alain's car there!'

'Don't worry,' soothed Danny. 'They're probably just continuing the wedding party.'

But Claire was already wrenching open the car door and racing across the uneven lawn. As she reached the steps of the front veranda, a dark figure appeared against the lighted doorway. A chill sense of foreboding clutched at Claire's stomach.

'Alain!' she cried. 'Where are my parents? What's going on?'

He was down the stairs in an instant and gripping her shoulders.

'Where have you been?' he demanded harshly. 'I've had men looking for you all over town for the last two hours.'

'But why?' she croaked. 'What's happened?'

'Your father's had another heart attack,' he said heavily.

She reeled and would have fallen if he had not caught her.

'He's not——?' she began.

'No! But it's serious.'

Raising one hand to her face, she shook her head distractedly.

'Where is he?' she demanded, her voice rising and growing more shrill. 'I must go to him! And Maman...oh, heavens, it's all my fault! I should never have gone out and left them.'

'Don't be absurd!' snapped Alain. 'It could have happened at any moment. And your mother's coping very well. I saw her safely aboard the ambulance myself.'

Claire gave him a dazed look.

'What were you doing here?' she asked.

'Eve phoned me as soon as she had called the ambulance. Luckily I arrived just before he went into cardiac arrest. But between us we gave him mouth to mouth and cardiopulmonary massage until the ambulance came.'

Claire shuddered.

'Thank you,' she choked.

He took her hand. There was nothing sexual in that warm contact, but Claire found it infinitely comforting. Another involuntary shudder went through her and she squeezed Alain's fingers tightly, gripping on to him as if he could save her from disaster. His hand gripped hers back for a brief moment, then he thrust her towards his car.

'Come on! Let's get moving,' he ordered curtly.

Danny was standing on the lawn and he came forward as they neared the Citroën.

'I heard everything,' he explained. 'Is there any way I can help?'

'No,' said Alain brusquely.

Danny took Claire's hand and squeezed it hard.

'Good luck, love,' he muttered. 'Let me know how it goes.' Then he ran to move his hire car so that Alain could get out of the driveway.

From that point onwards, the whole night seemed to dissolve into a whirling kaleidoscope of fractured images for Claire. The suburbs of Papeete with sulphur-yellow street-lights and stately palm trees. The polished floors and white lights and echoing voices of the hospital. And hours and hours of waiting in a small, bare room with shuttered windows and old copies of *Paris Match* lying on a table. Until shortly after dawn when slits of red-gold light filtered through the shutters and a grave-faced doctor came and asked for Madame Beaumont. Claire gripped Alain's hand again, unaware that she had suddenly turned as pale as the wall behind her. Oh, let him be all right, she prayed silently. Please, please, let Papa be all right. Tears pricked her eyes and spilt over on her cheeks as she watched her mother's blurred figure walk out of the room.

Eve was gone for several minutes and when she came back she was crying openly. A cold feeling went through Claire's entire body and she rose to her feet in sickening slow motion.

'He's dead, isn't he?' she said through frozen lips.

Somewhere, far off, she felt Alain's arm tighten protectively round her shoulders.

'Dead? No!' choked Eve exultantly. 'I'm only crying because it's such a blessed, blessed relief. He's regained consciousness and there's no sign of brain damage. Your Papa's going to live, Claire! He's going to live!'

They all went slightly crazy at the news, hugging each other and laughing. Claire came back to earth to find herself squeezed hard against Alain's muscular chest with the scent of his cologne in her nostrils and the warmth of his arms around her. Feeling suddenly self-conscious, she wriggled free and smiled at him uncertainly.

'Well, what do we do now?' she asked.

'I can drive you both back home, if you like,' suggested Alain.

'Not me,' replied Eve firmly. 'Although Roland is conscious, the doctors haven't allowed me in to see him yet and I'm not leaving until they do. But if you could take Claire home, Alain, that would be very kind.'

'But don't you want me to stay with you, Maman?' asked Claire.

'No, dear,' said her mother. 'It's no use. They won't let anyone else see Papa today and there are the chickens and the dog waiting to be fed at home.'

'Well, if you're sure,' agreed Claire doubtfully. 'You will get a taxi when you're ready to come home, won't you?'

'Yes, darling,' promised Eve. 'Now, off you go, both of you. And thank you, Alain. You were wonderful.'

'Maman's right, Alain,' Claire agreed in a strained voice. 'You were wonderful. I don't know what we would have done without you. You were so calm and dependable.'

His dark blue eyes met hers, with that intense, brooding look that seemed to mask some hidden sorrow or anger. Then he looked bleakly away and addressed his reply to Eve.

'I hope you'll always feel you can depend on me,' he said.

CHAPTER FIVE

SUNRISE was blazoning a banner of red-gold radiance across the lagoon as they sped home towards Point Cupid. At the summit, where the hotel lay hidden behind its shelter of luxuriant greenery, Alain drew off the road and stopped the car.

'What are you doing?' asked Claire in surprise.

'Getting out to watch the sunrise properly,' he replied. 'I always do when I have the chance.'

This statement surprised her. She was so used to thinking of Alain as a soulless businessman obsessed with blueprints and building permits and making money. Slamming his door, he came around to her side of the car.

'Come on,' he urged, holding out one lean, brown hand. 'It will do you good to realise that the world hasn't come to an end just yet.'

She let him lead her across to the small viewing platform where the panorama of land and sea was spread out below them. Birds warbled noisily in the orange canopies of the tulip trees, the air was fresh with the scent of flowers and down below the sea was changing colour from wild rose to palest blue. Alain's warm, strong arm draped itself around her shoulders and a strange pang went through her. He was so full of vitality and purpose, just like this luxuriant, tropical paradise that vibrated so insistently with life. She shuddered, unable to feel in harmony with either the man or the place.

'What is it?' he asked, looking down at her with searching blue eyes.

She shrugged, tried to smile and failed, bit her lip.

'It all seems too normal,' she complained. 'Too cheerful. Life going on as usual, just as if nothing had happened. When all the time my father might have died.'

'Oh, Claire,' he said impatiently. 'That's what life does. It goes on, no matter how miserable we may feel. Sickness, death, betrayal, none of those are enough to stop it, so we simply have to cope the best way we can. Just as well really. Keeping going and refusing to give in is the best remedy I know for unhappiness.'

There was a harsh undertone in his voice, as if he were speaking from bitter experience. Claire shot him a keen glance, taking in every detail of his brooding blue eyes, his twisted mouth, the way his lean fingers gripped the railing. He's been hurt badly at some time, she thought with piercing insight. And he's never really recovered, whatever he may say, so his fine advice didn't do him much good. Anyway it's all very well to talk about keeping going, but sometimes it seems an emotional impossibility. Like now, for instance. She caught her breath on a swift, uneven sob, not even certain of what was upsetting her most. Was it her father's illness or Alain's barely controlled antagonism?

'Stop that!' ordered Alain sharply. 'You can't help your father by worrying yourself sick. Look, Claire, you need something to take your mind off all this. I'll tell you what. Why don't we park the car at my house and go down the cliff track to your place? The walk will help you to unwind.'

'The cliff track?' echoed Claire with a flicker of unwilling interest. 'Is it still there? I thought you would have closed it when you built the hotel. I haven't been on it since I was a teenager.'

'Yes, it's still there,' agreed Alain. 'I had some handrails put in at the dangerous spots, but otherwise it should be just as you remember it.'

It was just as Claire remembered it. A dizzying downward track, fringed by orange lantana bushes and overhung by ropes of greenery, which nevertheless gave magnificent views of the ocean beneath. When they finally scrambled out among the coconut palms at the base of the cliff, she pushed her hair out of her eyes and smiled unsteadily.

'You're right,' she panted. 'I do feel better.'

A glimmer of an answering smile crossed Alain's face and then vanished, leaving his features as stormy as ever. Too wild, too fierce for mere conventional good looks, he exuded an aura of raw, masculine power and authority that made Claire feel suddenly breathless. He looked at her intently and for one heart-stopping moment, she thought he was going to drag her into his arms and kiss her. A strange, pulsating yearning swept through her at the thought. She felt acutely conscious not only of his powerful physical presence, but also of the emotional currents that surged between them. Some kind of struggle was clearly going on in Alain's innermost heart and she sensed the fierce urgency of his need for her in the way his gaze devoured her. But then he turned abruptly away and began striding along the dark volcanic sand near the water's edge.

'Come on,' he said over his shoulder. 'Let's get back to your house and make some breakfast. I'm hungry.'

He strode briskly along the beach and with a faint sigh Claire loped after him. But however much Alain might have wanted to shut her out, the atmosphere of the place worked insidiously to bring them together. Now and then they had to jump nimbly back to avoid a sudden rushing assault by a larger wave than usual. And once, when they mistimed it, they found themselves caught in a surge of cool, refreshing foam. Inevitably they shared a rueful smile and some of Claire's tension drained away. She let her thoughts drift, enjoying the caress of the salt-laden breeze on her face, the hiss and rush of the waves, the gleaming brilliance of the jade-green lagoon. Her breathing slowed and steadied and she felt a new sense of peace descend upon her.

'That's better,' said Alain brusquely. 'You've got some colour in your face again. Now once you've had something to eat you'll feel fine.'

She found his bossy, protective manner oddly reassuring. It was comforting to let someone else shoulder the burden while she let a healing vagueness wash over. When he pushed open the garden gate of her home, she was quite content to follow him to the back door and let him organise her.

'You feed the hens and the dog and I'll put the coffee on,' he instructed. 'Don't worry. I'll find my way around.'

Five minutes later she came back to find the kitchen filled with the fragrant aroma of percolating coffee. Alain was laying plates on the red-checked tablecloth, where Marie Rose's bouquet sat in splendour in a jug of water. Claire gave a low gasp and clapped her hand over her mouth.

'Marie Rose!' she exclaimed. 'I forgot all about her. I'll have to phone and tell her what's happened. But I don't even know where she is.'

Alain took her by the shoulders and pushed her ruthlessly into a chair.

'It's all under control,' he said. 'They left New York at one-fifty p.m. Eastern Time on Flight 684 headed for Paris. We'll phone them at their hotel when they arrive.'

Claire looked stunned.

'How on earth do you know all that?' she demanded. 'Are you clairvoyant?'

Alain shrugged impatiently.

'No, but you seem to forget that I was the best man,' he replied. 'I had to book all the tickets and see that they left on time, remember.'

So. Not clairvoyant, but merely efficient, practical, invaluable in an emergency. Claire gazed at Alain with a lump in her throat.

'I don't know how I can ever thank you——' she began, but he cut her off.

'Eat your waffles,' he said.

The waffles were crisp, hot, smothered in maple syrup. Claire ate two helpings of them, drank a glass of orange juice and a cup of strong, sweet coffee and looked across at Alain. And in that moment she found that the universe had changed. He still looked stern when his face was in repose. There were hollows in his cheeks and a tough, unyielding look about the sardonic mouth. And yet she knew now that he wasn't, and never could have been, the ogre she had once believed him. Brusque, unforgiving, capable of blazing anger, yes. But not heartless, not cruel. Beneath that grim exterior, Alain Charpentier was a warm and caring person, capable of infinite kindness. He caught her gaze upon him and smiled faintly. It was that smile, wary and fleeting, that completed the destruction of her heart. Staring at him with her lips parted and her heart thudding violently, Claire realised with piercing certainty that she loved him.

'Is something wrong?' he asked.

His voice with its sultry, smoky undertones unnerved her still further. Blushing fierily, she looked away and searched desperately for some harmless topic of conversation.

'I'm just wondering if there's anyone else I should phone about Papa,' she babbled. 'I know my aunts and uncles will need to hear the news, although I suppose that can wait. But——'

'Did your father have any tours to do today?' asked Alain.

Claire started. She had forgotten all about her father's tours.

'Yes, he probably did,' she agreed, running her fingers through her hair with a harassed gesture. 'But I've no idea where he would keep the passenger list. He's so disorganised.'

A lengthy hunt through the chaotic sitting-room and kitchen finally revealed a scrawled passenger list on the wrong side of a video loan slip held on the fridge door by a magnet. Claire groaned affectionately.

'Isn't that just like him?' she demanded, wrinkling her forehead. 'But he hasn't got any of the hotels written down, unless these weird initials mean something.'

'Give it to me,' instructed Alain, holding out his hand. 'May I use your phone?'

Within ten minutes he had it all sorted out.

'I've told one of my men from the hotel to take over for Roland until he's fit to work again,' he said. 'That way he won't lose income while he's sick, and Robert knows the routes well. He's filled in for him once before.'

Claire stared at him, appalled.

'But I can't possibly let you do that!' she protested. 'I'm sure this man must have work of his own to do at the hotel, hasn't he?'

'Well, yes, but——'

'But nothing!' insisted Claire. 'Oh, Alain, it's good of you. It's terribly, terribly generous, but I can't let some stranger take over my father's job, when it might be weeks before he's fit to work again himself. And what if there aren't enough bookings to pay Robert's wages?'

'Will you stop worrying about the damned wages?' thundered Alain. 'Let that be my concern!'

'No!' cried Claire, jumping to her feet. 'Alain, it's not fair that you should take on a burden like that. Look, I'd be grateful enough just for today, if Robert could do it. But after that, I'll have to make some arrangements of my own to deal with the problem. I'm not taking on outside help unless I know for sure that we can afford to pay for it. And before I can even guess at that, I'll have to find Papa's account books and figure out what's going on here.'

'You'll do nothing of the kind,' said Alain arrogantly.

Claire clamped her tongue between her teeth and counted to ten. At least she began counting to ten, but only reached three before she exploded.

'And why not?' she demanded, her eyes glinting dangerously.

'Because, hospitable and generous as he is, your father is also the most chaotic businessman this side of the Equator,' retorted Alain. 'I've done my best to help him, but he's got no more idea of accounting than a fish in the sea. Account books, indeed! Torn-up cardboard and the backs of old envelopes is more like it and even if you find those you won't be able to make head nor tail out of them. If you've got any worries about running your father's business while he's sick, you'd much better turn the whole thing over to me. At least I know what I'm doing.'

'You patronising——!' Claire broke off and took a rein on her temper. 'All right, Alain. I accept that you're trying to be helpful and it's kind of you, but it just won't do. It's my responsibility to sort out Papa's affairs, not yours.'

Alain's jaw set in a stubborn line.

'That's ridiculous,' he said. 'Just tell your mother that I'll deal with the business for as long as necessary. I'm sure she'll be only too happy to let me deal with it.'

I'm sure she will too, thought Claire with a sinking sensation. But I'm certainly not going to let an outsider see the kind of confusion my father can create. It would be far too humiliating. I'll just have to get it all sorted out myself.

'Well?' prompted Alain. 'Will you pass on the message?'

'I suppose so,' agreed Claire in exasperation. 'But why should you be troubled with our difficulties?'

'Sometimes I could shake you!' said Alain impatiently. 'Don't you realise that I'm only too glad to help? Nobody's ever really depended on me before and, to be honest, I rather like the sensation. Besides, your parents have made me feel far more welcome and valued than my own family ever did.'

Claire sank slowly back into her chair.

'Whatever do you mean?' she asked.

Alain paced moodily round the room, running his fingers through his hair.

'You don't want to hear my entire life story, do you?' he retorted with wry humour.

Claire frowned thoughtfully at him.

'Yes, as a matter of fact, I do,' she replied. 'Do you realise that I know nothing about you before you moved to Tahiti six years ago? Well, nothing but a few snippets of information that your aunt told me.'

Alain scowled.

'Denise?' he said. 'What did she tell you?'

Claire coloured as she remembered the juiciest item of gossip that Denise had passed on—the story of Alain's relationship to Nadine. Yet she didn't want to mention that—not only because it seemed too intimate and prying to have discussed such a matter, but also for the very simple reason that she felt like bursting into tears when she thought about it.

'N-nothing really. Just that your family owned a chain of hotels right across France. She made me feel that Marie Rose and I had a cheek to be breathing the same air as you.'

Alain gave a savage growl of laughter.

'That sounds about right,' he admitted. 'Denise suffers from the cruel delusion that money makes people more important and valuable than anything else on earth. She simply doesn't realise how worthless it really is.'

'Worthless?' echoed Claire with a comic grimace, looking down at the chipped coffee-mug in her hands and then out at the rusty bath still marooned on the lawn. 'I don't know about that. I'd say it has its uses!'

Alain sighed.

'Yes, it does,' he acknowledged. 'But it shouldn't rule people's lives as it does in Denise's case. Although I suppose I shouldn't be too hard on her. She did take Louise and me in as children when we had nowhere else to go.'

Claire stared at him in horror.

'Oh, no, you poor little things!' she said with ready sympathy. 'What happened? Did your parents die?'

Alain stretched his muscular brown arms and then gripped the back of a chair. The movement somehow reminded Claire of a panther, lurking in hiding and tensing itself for a spring.

'No,' he said, hunching one shoulder in a shrug. 'You can save your pity. Our parents didn't die, they simply got divorced. You've heard of custody battles over children, haven't you? Well, this was a custody battle with a difference. Neither of them wanted us, so they fought over who wouldn't keep us. In the end I suppose you could say they both won.'

'What happened?' asked Claire.

'Uncle Charles offered to take us,' said Alain. 'He was my mother's brother, but you couldn't possibly find two people less alike. Denise wasn't keen, but he insisted, so that's why I grew up feeling that Paul was more like my brother than my cousin.'

'How old were you when it happened?' she asked.

'I was six. Louise was only four and completely bewildered by it all. She cried for my mother every night for the first three months. I always felt I had to protect her after that.'

Claire flinched. It explained a lot. Like Alain's violent rage when he believed she was deliberately wrecking Louise's marriage. And the way he usually seemed so stern and unapproachable.

'Didn't you ever see your parents after that?' she asked.

'Once or twice a year,' he said indifferently. 'But they weren't parents any more, just strangers. A glamorous woman who wouldn't let us sit on her furniture when we visited and a cold, self-contained man, who was too busy to speak to us when we phoned him. My mother's still alive, you know. She lives in Marseilles and she's on her fifth husband and her third facelift. My father died of a cerebral haemorrhage from overwork two years ago.'

Claire's tender heart was touched. Reaching out, she squeezed his hand hesitantly.

'Oh, Alain, I'm so sorry,' she murmured.

His blue eyes looked cold and hard and unforgiving.

'Don't be,' he said grimly. 'None of it matters to me any more.'

'But that's the worst thing of all!' burst out Claire indignantly. 'Don't you see that you'll wind up just like your father if you're not careful? Cold and self-contained and too caught up in your work to bother with people?'

Alain glared at her.

'Is that how you see me?' he grated, seizing her by the wrist and hauling her out of her chair.

She found herself dragged up hard against him. So close that she could hear the angry thudding of his heart through his thin shirt and feel the heat radiating from his body in waves. A jolt of emotion that was halfway between rage and desire surged through her.

'Yes!' she cried defiantly. 'It is!'

And then fairness made her pause.

'Well, it used to be,' she muttered.

Alain scowled.

'And why the sudden change of opinion?' he demanded sarcastically.

Claire looked him straight in the eye.

'Because you were so kind about my father,' she said with a catch in her voice.

A momentary spark of warmth kindled in his features, then his face was suddenly bleak again.

'Don't make too much out of that,' he warned. 'I only did what any decent neighbour would do, but it doesn't change anything fundamental about my character, Claire. Or yours.'

'It does,' she insisted, clutching at his arms. 'I always thought you were really harsh and unfeeling and far too ready to judge other people, but I was wrong, Alain. I know I was. And I'm sorry I ever thought that about you. I'm sure you're a really warm person underneath, except that——'

'Expect that what?' demanded Alain.

'Except that you're afraid to risk being hurt, so you never really get involved with anyone,' she finished in a rush.

His grip tightened on her arms and for a moment she thought he was going to kiss her. But instead, he thrust her savagely away and strode across the room.

'And what made you think I was so cold and hard and self-contained in the first place?' he demanded, turning back to face her.

A stab of dismay went through her as she saw the smouldering intensity of his gaze. However kind Alain might be in an emergency, it was clear that nothing had really changed between them. His contempt for her was as bitter as ever.

'Well, what was it?' he snapped.

Biting her lip, she struggled to explain. But at the mere thought of that hideous scene six years before, her nerve failed her. She could not even bear to mention it for fear of reawakening his anger.

'I-I don't know,' she stammered lamely.

'Don't lie, Claire,' he said in a hard voice. 'It's because of what I said to you when I found out about Marcel, isn't it?'

At the mere mention of that name, she winced and turned her head as if he had struck her.

'Don't mention him,' she begged hoarsely. 'Please. I can't bear it.'

His gaze held hers, brooding and relentless.

'Why not?' he demanded. 'Are you still in love with him?'

Claire felt the old, familiar horror rise inside her. Her whole body stiffened and she made an angry, convulsive gesture with one hand, as if she could push the memories away.

'No, of course not!' she said through her teeth. 'After six years, how could I keep loving someone who hurt me so badly?'

'It's not impossible,' replied Alain grimly. 'But am I to assume that you now regard the whole thing as a sordid little encounter which should never have happened?'

'Yes,' choked Claire.

'Then why did you think that what I did was so cruel, so unreasonable?' demanded Alain.

Her eyes filled with stinging tears.

'I'll cry if I try to talk about it,' she warned.

'So cry,' he ordered brutally. 'There are worse things than crying. Worse pain.'

'OK,' she gasped. 'I'll tell you why.'

She paused for a moment, fighting down tears.

'You really set yourself up as judge, jury and executioner, didn't you?' she accused. 'Look, I accept that you were shocked and horrified when you found me with Marcel, but you wouldn't listen to anything I had to say. But I honestly didn't know he was married, Alain, and I felt as if my whole world had fallen apart when you told me. You can't imagine the heartache, the sense of betrayal I felt when you burst in on us that afternoon.'

'Oh, yes, I can,' muttered Alain, half to himself.

'You can't!' cried Claire. 'All you were thinking about was how upset Louise would be and how angry you were. But you never gave a thought to me, did you? How do you think I felt when I found out that Marcel was married? Whatever you choose to believe, Alain, I was just as much a victim of that man as your sister was. And it didn't help to have you telling me I'd have to leave the country, not to mention calling me a whore and——'

Her voice broke and she pressed her fist against her mouth. Alain watched her in silence for a moment. Then abruptly he crossed the floor and drew her shaking body into his arms.

'Come here,' he said roughly.

He held her until her trembling ceased and then drew out a clean handkerchief and dried her eyes.

'Perhaps I did jump to some hasty conclusions about you,' he admitted. 'I certainly wasn't at my clearest and calmest that day. But I knew your mother's sister had already invited you to come and stay in Sydney. And I really thought it was best for everybody concerned if you left Tahiti a bit early. Particularly since Louise was due to arrive from Paris at any moment. I thought the whole thing could be far more easily hushed up if you vanished off the island.'

'Hushed up?' retorted Claire incredulously. 'You swore you were going to tell my parents what I'd done.'

Alain gave an exasperated sigh.

'Well, I probably did,' he agreed. 'But you can't possibly have taken me seriously!'

'Can't I?' flashed back Claire. 'I spent weeks crying myself to sleep every night in Sydney, terrified that my parents were going to ring up and disown me. And, even when I finally got over that fear, I still couldn't face going home to Tahiti. I was so scared of you.'

Alain snorted.

'You don't seriously expect me to believe that you stayed away for six years, just because you were frightened to death of me, do you?' he demanded.

Claire smiled sadly and paced across to the kitchen sink. Restlessly she picked up a glass tumbler, set it down again, placed a perfectly clean teaspoon in the washing-up water.

'Oddly enough,' she said hoarsely, 'that's very close to being the truth. Oh, I eventually realised that you probably didn't have the power to get me deported if I came back. But I knew you did have the power to hurt and humiliate me. And my family. So I never thought it was worth the risk until Marie Rose persuaded me.'

Alain was staring at her with disbelief written all over his face.

'And that's really why you didn't come back?' he asked sceptically.

'Yes,' said Claire simply. 'Why else do you think I would abandon my home and family for so long?'

He let out his breath in an impatient sigh.

'Because I thought you were so intoxicated with fame and success that you didn't give a damn about them any more!' he replied.

Claire flinched.

'Thank you,' she said.

'Look, I'm sorry,' muttered Alain, running his fingers through his hair again. 'The truth is that the whole thing is a hopeless mess. Like some nuclear accident that's still sending out its poisonous radiation years after-wards. But I don't think there's anything to be gained by probing into the past any further, Claire. Maybe you're telling the truth, but how can I be sure of that?'

Claire clenched her fists so hard that her nails dug into her palms. It hurt her unbearably to think that Alain would never trust her again.

'Can't you just give me the benefit of the doubt?' she demanded. 'Can't you let go of the past and give us a chance to be friends?'

'Friends?' echoed Alain in an odd voice. 'I'm not at all sure that I want to be your friend, Claire.'

'Then what do you want from me?' she blazed.

He advanced towards her with an intent, glittering look in his eyes and caught her by the arms. Thrusting his face so close to hers that she could see the veins throbbing at his temples, he glared down at her.

'I don't know what I want from you,' he snarled. 'That's the whole trouble. But maybe what I want is this.'

His merciless fingers stilled and then tightened. Almost lifting her off her feet with the intensity of his grip, he treated her to a long, demanding kiss. Dizzy with need, she closed her eyes and surrendered to the thrill of his warm mouth on hers, the hard, intoxicating pressure of his arms imprisoning her body. Shivers of sensation coursed through her and, when he sensually stroked the swelling contour of her breast, she whimpered softly and thrust herself against him.

'Oh, Alain,' she gasped. 'Alain, Alain.'

Conscious only of the shallow rhythm of their mingled breathing, Claire lifted her mouth to his. He kissed her again with a ferocity that terrified and exalted her. She felt his muscles bunch and harden beneath the skin as he hauled her against him and a throbbing ache of desire spread through her loins. At that moment he could have taken her and she would have offered no resistance, would have gloried in her surrender, but he did not do it. Instead, with a sharp, sudden intake of breath, he thrust her away from him.

Her eyes flew open and she stared at him. His face looked dark and strange and she could not read his expression.

'No. Not now. Not here,' he muttered, striding away from her towards the door.

'Alain, wait!' she cried.

He turned and stared at her with stormy, blue eyes.

'Well?' he demanded.

A tremor of misgiving went through her.

'Can we be friends?' she asked uncertainly.

'Friends?' His laugh was harsh, ugly, tormented. 'Yes, I suppose you could say so.'

She darted after him and clutched his arm, possessed by a sudden fear that she would never see him again.

'Then you'll be coming back?' she persisted.

'Oh, yes,' he growled. 'I'll be coming back. It seems your attraction is just as potent as it ever was.'

Left alone, Claire sank down into a chair and buried her face in her hands. Her lips still tingled from Alain's kiss and her whole body felt as if it were on fire with longing. Yet this aching sense of need brought her little joy. From the first moment Alain had met her at the airport, she had felt a current of physical tension between them, as unpredictable and dramatic as summer lightning. Claire had tried to dismiss it as mere lust, the random spark of attraction that could blaze so violently between man and woman and mean so little. But now she felt with bitter certainty that it was more than that, at least for her. She loved Alain Charpentier and she wanted love in return. A deep, powerful, total commitment that would allow them to weather the storms of life side by side. Not just a meaningless sexual encounter, however intense. But was Alain likely to offer her that commitment?

'Of course not!' she said aloud, slamming her hands down on the table and rising to her feet. 'Don't be such a fool, Claire! He doesn't love you; all he wants to do is jump into bed with you! And all the while, he's probably planning to marry Nadine anyway. About the only good thing to be said for him is that at least he doesn't lie about his motives, the way Marcel did.'

Biting her thumb, she paced restlessly across to the window and stared out over the garden and the tranquil lagoon. Her movement caught the attention of the dog, who was lounging in the shade of a bush, licking her paws. Jumping up, the tan mongrel shook herself, picked up a frisbee in her mouth and appeared at the back door, hopefully wagging her tail.

'No, Sissy!' said Clair, smiling reluctantly as she looked at the animal through the screen door. 'I don't have time to play games. I've got to think about important things, like what to do about Alain. And how to get my father's business affairs in order and whether to get special leave from my job until Papa is better. Or whether to give up my job altogether and just stay here. I can't play games with you.'

Sissy cocked her head on one side. Her huge, melting brown eyes were full of pathos and she whined reproachfully.

'Oh, all right then, you little wretch!' said Claire, giving in. 'But only for five minutes, mind.'

Somehow, once she was outside throwing the toy for the dog, she felt herself growing gradually calmer. The garden was as beautiful as ever with its blazing orange tulip tree, its tangled hedges of red ginger and yellow hibiscus and the dappled shade beneath the banyan tree. When at last Claire stretched lazily and flung herself into a chair on the patio, some of her misery had dissipated.

'Maybe it will all work out, Sissy,' she murmured. 'Papa will get better, Alain will realise that I'm not so dreadful after all, Nadine will go back to Paris, I'll know instinctively what to do about my job and everyone will live happily ever after. Don't you think so?'

Sissy thrust her soft, damp muzzle into Claire's hand and whined agreement. Claire chuckled.

'Well, it's nice to have someone who thinks I'm wonderful, no matter what,' she said, fondling the dog's long, floppy ears. 'Now I really have got to go and sort out Papa's business papers before my mother comes home. If I don't get it organised, I know she'll insist that I hand everything over to Alain and I'm not prepared to do that. But at least I feel brave enough to tackle it now.'

Yet within half an hour Claire's bravery had evaporated. Alain was right about her father's book-keeping system and she had a confused pile of makeshift documents on the desk in front of her. Used envelopes, supermarket dockets, the top of a cereal packet and wrapping paper from some decidedly greasy French fries had all been used to record accounts paid and money received. And no doubt there were more of these impromptu papers scattered around the house. But what troubled Claire more than any of this was a single, beautifully typed, signed and legally witnessed document which showed that Roland Beaumont owed Alain Charpentier more than a million French Pacific francs. With a chill feeling in her stomach, Claire wondered how on earth the debt was ever to be repaid.

It was late afternoon when her mother returned. Claire had been dozing in her room, but woke to the sound of a car pulling up outside. Yawning, she made her way to the front door just in time to see her mother waving vigorously as the car reversed again.

'Hello, dear,' said Eve, kissing her cheek. 'That was your father's cousin Maea. Wasn't it sweet of her to give me a lift home? And guess what else? She's invited me to stay with her until Roland has recovered enough to come home. Then live right near the hospital and it will be so much more convenient for me. She's coming back later to pick me up.'

'How is Papa?' asked Claire, steering her mother inside.

A tremor passed across Eve's features, then she pressed her lips determinedly together.

'Much better,' she said brightly. 'But of course they can't be sure that it won't happen again. Oh, Claire, I don't know how I'll manage if it does. If you and Alain hadn't been here...'

She left the sentence unfinished.

'Come on, Maman,' urged Claire. 'Come and sit down and I'll make you a cup of tea.'

Any thought she might have had about discussing Roland's debt to Alain vanished instantly from her mind. It was obvious that her mother was close to breaking point and she didn't want to worry her any further. All the same, she made up her mind to tackle Alain on the subject the next time she saw him.

She did not have long to wait. Ten minutes later, as they sat drinking their tea on the veranda, Alain arrived. Eve jumped up and kissed him on both cheeks.

'I can't tell you how grateful I am for all you did last night,' she said unsteadily.

'Nonsense,' replied Alain, hugging her hard. 'It was nothing. But how is he, Eve?'

Alain and Claire both listened attentively as Eve recited everything the doctors had told her. At one point she broke off and her eyes filled with tears, but then she recovered enough to explain her plans about staying with Maea.

'That sounds very sensible,' agreed Alain. 'And you're not to worry about the tour business, Eve. Claire and I have everything under control.'

'Oh, thank you both,' sighed Eve. 'I only wish that Claire could stay on. I know it's selfish of me to say it, but I've missed her dreadfully since she went away and it will be worse now that Marie Rose isn't here. Still, you've got your job to do, pet, and we're all very proud of the way you do it.'

Claire swallowed the lump that rose in her throat and looked from Alain to her mother. Alain's eyes were narrowed and watchful and she could make nothing of the brooding look on his face. Yet some inner magnetism drew her so powerfully to him that she almost reached out and touched him. In that moment she knew with painful certainty that if she stayed on in Tahiti she would be taking an enormous risk. Sooner or later the smouldering sexual heat between them would blaze up and she was likely to be very badly hurt. But Marie Rose was right. If she ever wanted to find love, she couldn't keep running scared for the rest of her life. And, in any case, her mother needed her. In that moment she reached a decision.

'I'm not going back to Australia,' she said calmly. 'I'm giving up my job and staying here.'

There was a moment's shocked silence. Then Eve began to protest.

'Oh, now, sweetheart, I didn't mean that. I couldn't ask you to do anything of the kind just because I'm selfish enough to want you here.'

'You're not selfish and you're not asking me to do it,' replied Claire swiftly. 'I'm offering and that's completely different. Anyway I want to stay here. I'm sick of travelling and I always get homesick while I'm away.'

'But think of the wonderful salary you make,' urged Eve.

'I don't care about the salary!' cried Claire impatiently.

'And you're so famous,' protested Eve.

'I'm not interested in being famous!' retorted Claire. 'I'm interested in being with the people I love when they need me and in being happy. What's wrong with that?'

Alain had taken no part in the discussion, but he leant forward in his chair like a spectator at Wimbledon as the volley of discussion flew back and forth. Now he intervened.

'What will you do if you stay here, Claire?' he asked.

'I'll run Papa's tours until he's well enough to do it himself,' she replied.

Eve sighed.

'I don't know, dear,' she said, shaking her head. 'Of course I'd love to have you here, but I'm afraid you might regret it later. Couldn't you get special leave from your job, so that you could go back if you changed your mind?'

'I'll do it that way if it will make you any happier, Maman,' agreed Claire. 'But I'm sure I won't change my mind.'

At that moment they were interrupted by the toot of a car horn. It was Maea, who had come to fetch Eve. There was a chaotic flurry of activity while Eve packed a bag, then the two older women departed, leaving Alain and Claire alone.

'Are you seriously planning to give up a high-powered television job and settle permanently in Tahiti?' asked Alain, frowning at her across the table.

'Yes,' said Claire simply.

Now that the decision had finally been made, she felt an amazing sense of lightness and freedom, as if a terrible burden had been lifted from her shoulders. She smiled.

'Won't you miss the glamour and the jet-set lifestyle?' he asked.

She shook her head emphatically.

'No!' she exclaimed. 'In fact, I think I'll enjoy doing Papa's tours and trying to get the business on its feet. Besides, there are such wonderful places in the interior of the island that most people never see. I can't wait to show them off to visitors.'

'So you're really prepared to drive a four-wheel vehicle over rugged terrain and get covered in mud and

eaten up by mosquitoes, when you could be staying in
glamorous hotels in London and New York?' persisted
Alain.

Claire gave a gurgle of laughter.

'Oh, don't make me sound so heroic!' she protested.
'I'll take my insect repellent along, I promise. And it
really will be fun, Alain.'

'It's odd,' muttered Alain, half to himself. 'I'd always
thought the good life was really important to you, but
perhaps I was wrong. Well, if there's anything I can do
to help you, just ask me, won't you? I've got a pretty
good idea of how Roland was running the business.'

A shadow passed across Claire's face.

'That reminds me,' she said. 'There is something I
need to ask you. I want to know about the money Papa
owes you.'

The friendly warmth vanished from Alain's face to be
replaced by a forbidding scowl.

'So you've been prying into that, have you?' he demanded. 'I might have known. Well, let me tell you,
Claire, it's none of your damned business!'

'It certainly is my business if I'm the one who's going
to repay it,' insisted Claire.

'You don't have to repay it, so that's an end to the
matter,' snapped Alain.

'No, it isn't!' cried Claire. 'I'll have to get my father
to sign a power of attorney so I can carry on his business
while he's ill and that will give me a full legal right and
duty to deal with his debts. So I want to know why he
borrowed the money and when the repayment is due.
There was no date given in that document.'

Alain sighed impatiently.

'You obstinate little...' he breathed. 'All right, I'll
tell you why. Roland borrowed the money from me because he wanted to give Marie Rose a big wedding.'

'And you agreed, knowing that he had no hope of repaying it?' cried Claire hotly. 'I think that's outrageous. You should never have let him do it.'

'*Ichi, ni, san, shi, go* ...' muttered Alain under his breath.

'What's that supposed to mean?' demanded Claire.

'I'm just counting up to ten in Japanese while I resist the urge to strangle you!' retorted Alain.

'I see,' sneered Claire. 'Well, that's one way of changing the subject.'

'I am not changing the subject,' growled Alain. 'It's just that you make me so angry I could explode. Do you seriously think I had any intention of asking your father for repayment of that loan?'

'So what was the point of having a signed agreement about it then?' countered Claire.

'Look,' said Alain impatiently, 'it was obvious from the start that a big wedding was beyond Roland's means, so I offered to pay for it myself. After all, Paul is like a brother to me and I would have been happy to do it, but your father wouldn't hear of it. He has his pride. So I offered him a loan, knowing that he'd never be able to pay me back and not expecting it. That way we were both happy.'

'Well, I'm not!' insisted Claire. 'I have my pride too and, the way I see it, that's a debt that my family owes to you and I intend to pay it.'

'I don't want your money!' thundered Alain.

'Well, you're getting it whether you want it or not!' retorted Claire.

They sat glaring at each other across the table with their chins thrust out and their eyes blazing. Then Claire looked down and cleared her throat.

'The only thing is that I may have to ask you to wait a while,' she mumbled. 'I have a flat in Sydney which I'll try and sell, but it may take a while——'

'Don't be so damned ridiculous!' said Alain through gritted teeth. 'Do you have that document your father signed?'

'Y-yes, it's inside,' stammered Claire.

'Get it for me.'

She returned a moment later with a folder, which she handed to Alain. He opened it, took out the document, perused it silently and then ripped it to shreds.

'That should take care of that!' he said with satisfaction.

Claire sat gaping.

'You can't do that!' she wailed.

'I already have,' pointed out Alain.

'I'll stick it together!' she threatened wildly, snatching at the torn fragments.

But Alain was too quick for her. His lean brown hand closed over hers and ruthlessly turned her clenched fist over. Then, as easily as if he were unfurling the petals of a flower, he prised her fingers apart and picked the shreds of paper out of them. With a bored expression he stuffed them into the pocket of his shorts.

'Your honesty does you credit,' he drawled lazily. 'But I won't allow you to ruin yourself out of stupid pride, Claire. Now tell me, when do you plan to start doing these tours?'

She sat silently for a moment, her shoulders heaving as she fought for breath. It was humiliating to be beaten in such an absurd contest of strength and she could not miss the gleam of amusement in Alain's narrowed blue eyes.

'I don't know,' she said stormily, tossing her head. 'As soon as possible, I suppose.'

Alain smiled with infuriating smugness.

'Well, you'll need to know the route before you do anything else,' he said. 'I'll pick you up at eight o'clock tomorrow morning and take you on the tour myself.'

CHAPTER SIX

CLAIRE woke early the next morning with a pleased sense of anticipation. For a moment she lay staring at the ripples of sunlight dancing on her bedroom wall, then memory came surging back. Of course. Alain was taking her on the inland tour today. In spite of her various worries, a surge of excitement bubbled up inside her. For the first time she really felt convinced that everything was going to end happily. Her boss in Sydney had granted her extra leave from her job. Her father had spoken to her on the phone and was doing well. She had contacted Marie Rose, who had taken the news with her usual sturdy common sense. And Alain, while he might be arrogant and infuriating, was obviously going to do all he could to help her. Claire was singing light-heartedly when at last she padded along to the shower. But not for long.

'Oooh!' she gasped, as a hail of freezing water shot her in the back.

Five minutes later as she stood towelling her hair in the kitchen and watching the coffee bubble, Claire was still covered in goose bumps. A knock at the door caught her by surprise as she stood rubbing her hands together and blowing on them.

'What? Shivering in the tropics?' demanded Alain incredulously, as she opened the glass door. 'I don't believe it.'

Claire giggled.

'You would if you'd washed your hair under our shower,' she assured him. 'I'm sure that thermostat has packed up again and something tells me Papa is never going to get his ticket as a plumber. Well, never mind that. Why didn't you come to the front entrance?'

'I did,' said Alain drily. 'But your doorbell's not working either.'

'Oh, dear,' groaned Claire. 'I can see there are a few things I'll have to get organised around here.'

'If you give me a list of what needs to be done, I'll see to it for you,' offered Alain.

Claire stiffened.

'There's no need,' she said in a small, tight voice.

'Just as you like,' replied Alain with a shrug. 'Any chance of a cup of coffee before we leave?'

Thankful for something to do, she poured him a cup of fragrant black coffee. As they drank, she watched him covertly. She felt ashamed of being so prickly, but her family's comparative poverty embarrassed her and made her feel defensive, especially when Alain had already done so much for them. And yet deep down, she could not help admiring the careless generosity that made him tear up a loan agreement and offer to take on her burdens. If only he loved her as she did him, she would accept gratefully. As it was, pride would not allow her to owe him anything.

'Well, are you ready, then?' asked Alain, draining his cup.

Claire stood up and nodded.

'Yes,' she said, feeling in her pocket for the keys to the four-wheel-drive vehicle.

'You look very nice in that outfit,' said Alain, glancing down over her trim white blouse and yellow shorts. 'But you'll need a jacket to wear up on Mount Marau. And a swimsuit if you want to go in the pool at the Faarumai Falls.'

He himself was dressed in blue shorts and a striped polo shirt, but he had an expensive-looking beige windbreaker slung carelessly under one arm.

'All right,' agreed Claire. 'Just a jiffy.'

As they left Papeete behind them and headed up into the hills, she felt a marvellous sense of freedom sweep through her. Alain had insisted on driving, so that she was able to enjoy the breathtaking views as the shoreline dropped steadily away behind them.

'Now, when you get off the tarmac on to the dirt road up here, it's very important to get out of your vehicle and turn on the four-wheel-drive,' announced Alain. 'Never, never forget to do it, because these mountain roads are very dangerous, especially in wet weather. And if you go over the edge, it's a very long way down. Are you listening to me?'

'Yes, sir!' said Claire meekly, dragging herself away from contemplating the panorama below.

'All right. Well, hop out and I'll show you how to change over to four-wheel-drive,' ordered Alain. 'Unfortunately in the older models like this you have to get out of the car and engage the hubs on the front wheels to do it. That can be a damned nuisance in the middle of a tropical downpour, but don't ever be tempted to neglect it. I don't want you going over the edge of a precipice. Is that clear?'

'Yes!' agreed Claire impatiently.

She sighed as she followed Alain out of the car. In her opinion he was making entirely too much fuss about the four-wheel-drive, but no doubt it was all part of his complex personality.

'Does everything you're involved in have to be perfect?' she complained, as he crouched down beside the wheel.

His dark eyebrows drew together in an arrogant frown.

'Yes,' he replied curtly. 'I like to feel that I have things under control, that everything will work the way I want it. Is there anything wrong with that?'

There was a challenging note in his voice and Claire felt uncomfortable under his scrutiny. She shrugged.

'No-o,' she admitted. 'Probably not, if you're only dealing with four-wheel-drives, but what about when it comes to people? Do you apply that principle to them too?'

A smile twisted Alain's lips into a momentary sneer.

'Unfortunately I don't seem to have the same success at making people behave the way I want,' he retorted. 'Now, all you have to do is turn this knob, see?'

She knelt beside him and peered at the knob on the hub cap. If they had been lovers, she would have slipped her arm around his waist and laid her head briefly against his shoulder. For a moment she was tempted to do it anyway. She could almost feel his warmth and the hardness of his arm coming down to grip her. A shudder went through her and she stepped hastily back.

'Yes. I see. Thank you,' she said jerkily.

A look of grim amusement flashed across his face as if he had read her thoughts. Then he rose to his feet.

'We'd better get moving,' he announced. 'We have a lot of ground to cover.'

Claire's thoughts were whirling furiously as the vehicle took off again, carrying them up a sheer hillside, where market gardens were hewn out of the steep red earth. She had always loved these trips into the interior of the island as a child, but now she scarcely noticed the scenery that was unfolding around her. Down to the right, the land fell away in a precipitous green blur until it collided with the sea far below. To her left was the rainforest, lush and tangled, with occasional rampant bursts of pink and orange lantana or delicate green spider ferns. The sound of running water assaulted her ears above the grinding roar of the car's engine and sunlight flashed intermittently through the windscreen in a weird Morse code of light and shadow. Yet Claire noticed little of this. Her attention was completely taken up by the man who sat hunched over the wheel, sending the ve-

hicle hurtling up the mountainside in controlled bursts
of hard driving.

Alain's whole posture seemed to radiate energy, power
and a bitter, consuming frustration. Claire had no clear
idea of what impelled him so violently, but she had her
suspicions. Her own body was vibrating like a tautly
stretched string at the realisation of his nearness. That
brief, unfulfilling kiss the previous day had woken a
hunger in her that clamoured for satisfaction and she
was willing to bet that Alain was suffering in the same
way. Desire, after all, was no respecter of persons. The
fierce, voracious need that made her want to trail her
fingers teasingly down Alain's hard, muscular thigh was
probably tormenting him in exactly the same fashion.
And the fact that she loved him with an aching sweetness
that thrilled through her in waves, while he in all prob-
ability still despised her, really had nothing to do with
it. It was all just a cosmic joke, nature's little trick to
ensure the survival of the species. Nothing more than a
primitive instinct, in fact. But perhaps primitive instincts had quite a lot to be said for them? In an earlier
and more primitive time, wouldn't Alain simply have led
her into the jungle and taken her? The thought sent such
a sharp quiver of longing through her that she caught
her breath.

'What's wrong?' growled Alain.

'N-nothing,' she replied hastily.

But everything was wrong. She admitted that to herself
when they climbed out of the vehicle on the summit of
Mount Marau. It was unexpectedly chilly up here, with
razor-sharp mountain peaks looming out of the drifting
fog and an icy breeze that tugged at her hair and sent
it flying in long, dark skeins across her face. She wished
that she hadn't come or that things were different between her and Alain so that she could huddle laughing
into his embrace and enjoy the exhilaration of this eyrie
in the clouds. Yet Alain showed no sign of wanting to

embrace her. Instead he hunched his shoulders, dug his fists deep into the pockets of his windbreaker and jerked his head towards the plunging abysses and jagged green peaks in front of them.

'Well, there you are,' he shouted above the breeze. 'Tahiti's Grand Canyon. And, after you've shown the tourists that, I suggest you take them down to sea-level and thaw them out. You can always tell them a few stories about explorers and cannibals on the way.'

Perhaps to cover his own disquiet, he did exactly this, and Claire was fascinated to find out how much he actually knew about Tahiti's history. As he sent the car hurtling round the hairpin bends, he talked about the voyages of Cook and Bougainville as vividly as if he had first seen the islands from the crow's nest of a sailing ship.

'What made you settle in Tahiti, Alain?' asked Claire curiously. 'Didn't you like France?'

Alain's eyes narrowed keenly, as if he were staring down a long tunnel into the past.

'No, it wasn't that,' he murmured. 'I still have business interests in Paris and I fly there quite often. And enjoy it. But Tahiti seems to have reached out and assaulted me from the very first day I set foot here. It was a total culture shock, coming from the roar of traffic and the throng of people to this incredible jewel of a place. In a way I resented it.'

He stopped abruptly, as if he had said too much.

'Why?' asked Claire swiftly.

Alain drummed his fingers on the steering wheel.

'Does it matter?' he retorted.

'Yes,' said Claire slowly. 'Look, Alain, I don't want to pry, I'm only trying to understand the way you feel about things that are important to you. It seems crazy to me that we've been through things like my father's heart attack together and yet I still don't really know you. I always end up talking silly small talk with you and I hate conversations like that. But you don't have to talk to me if you'd rather not.'

Alain was silent for a moment, scowling at the road ahead. Then suddenly he spoke in a curiously clipped monotone.

'Well, if you must know,' he said, 'I resented Tahiti because, once I arrived here, my life seemed to change in ways I couldn't control and it alarmed me. I felt torn in two directions, because I knew I'd have to make a choice between the old life and the new. And being in love didn't make it any easier.'

He darted her a brief, slanting look that was cool and almost hostile. Claire's heart began to pound violently. What on earth did he mean? Was he talking about his broken engagement or was Marie Rose right? Had Alain really been in love with her, Claire Beaumont, six years ago? The mere thought made her dizzy with hope and terror. Yet surely he wouldn't be talking so calmly if that was what he meant? She must stop leaping to such ridiculous conclusions. What a fool she would make of herself if she weren't careful!

'In love?' she croaked, desperately trying to conceal her agitation. 'Oh, you mean with Nadine?'

Alain's gaze steadied on the approaching outskirts of the town.

'No, not with Nadine,' he said wryly. 'Although that might have made things simpler. With somebody else, but it's not important now. Look, shall we drive to the Arahoho blowhole on our way to the falls? I'm not sure whether your father includes it, but it might make an interesting visit for your tourists.'

The thunderous tumult of Claire's pulses gradually quietened as they drove south on the coast road. For one wild, intoxicating moment she had thought Alain was telling her obliquely that he had once loved her, although, as she watched his granite profile, that interpretation seemed less and less likely. Her turmoil slowly ebbed away, but her exhilaration vanished with it. She was conscious only of a bleak, twisting misery when at last Alain parked the car and led her along to the blowhole.

'There, don't you think they'd like that?' he asked, as a sudden jet of spray shot high into the air, sending them darting back out of range.

'I suppose so,' said Claire.

Normally she would have delighted in the caress of the moist sea breeze, the lavender-blue hues of the water and the dark volcanic rocks with their scuttling crabs and salamanders. But now she found herself possessed by a fierce impatience. She wanted the trip over and done with, so that she no longer had to endure the torment of being close to Alain without any hope of ever being closer.

'Can't we go?' she asked.

His head jerked up sharply, almost as if she had slapped his face, but he stepped back from the viewing platform readily enough.

'Yes, of course,' he said. 'I don't want to bore you. We'll just make a quick visit to the waterfall and then I'll take you home.'

Yet Claire felt as if there were electrical currents pulsing in the air between them as Alain drove along the leafy track leading to the falls. Once she caught his gaze on her and turned away, blushing hotly. It was a relief when he parked the car and led the way down an uneven path towards the sound of rushing water. Claire stopped, entranced.

'Isn't that beautiful?' she breathed.

Ahead of them was a sheer cliff of craggy, dark rock, covered with clinging ferns and spongy green mosses, everywhere except in the direct path of the falls. Craning her neck, Claire saw how the water hurtled over a sharp rampart at the top, bounded from crag to crag and finally

splintered into numerous silver showers in the pool
below.

'We can change in the hut,' said Alain.

Claire followed his gaze and saw a small thatched hut
set on the rocks a few metres from the water's edge. It
was open-sided with no separate partition for men and
women. Her throat constricted.

'I'm not sure that I want to swim——' she began, but
Alain cut her off.

'Shy?' he asked incredulously. 'Surely not, Claire? But
I promise to turn my back if that's what's worrying you.'

It seemed more dignified to give in than to argue.
Scarlet with embarrassment, Claire followed Alain into
the hut. Draping a voluminous beach towel around her,
she stripped off with quick, furtive movements and began
fumbling her way into her bikini. This was not made
any easier by the fact that a large, juicy mosquito was
whining around her legs and the floor of the hut was
uneven and pebbly. By the time she was ready, Alain
had already disappeared over the rocks and was wading
into the pool.

Claire picked her way gingerly across the rough ground
and stood watching him. He was built like an athlete
with wide shoulders, narrow hips and powerful back
muscles and she could not suppress an instinctive flutter
of excitement at the sight of him. As he reached the main
cascade at the foot of the cliff, he plunged his head under
the rushing water and then turned around, raising his
arms to brush his wet hair back from his face. With a
hail of white spray drumming off his brown shoulders,
the dark hair on his chest and underarms lying sleek and
flat and the taut, muscular outline of his solar plexus in
sharp relief, he looked like a Greek god. Claire found
her gaze wandering to the arrow of dark hair which vanished into his navy bathing trunks and looked
hastily away.

'Come on in,' he shouted. 'The water's fine once you get used to it.'

But that was an exaggeration, as Claire soon found out. She let out a squeal of shock as she entered the pool.

'You lie like a rug!' she cried accusingly. 'It might be fine for polar bears, but not for humans.'

'Oh, stop squeaking and come under the falls,' ordered Alain. 'You'll soon get used to it.'

The water was too shallow for any real swimming and the bottom was covered with large, uneven rocks, so that progress was difficult. But, crouching low and uttering stifled gasps of cold and surprise, Claire made her way across to join Alain. The moment she reached the foot of the cliff, he reached out one strong, brown hand and pulled her under the waterfall. She gave a cry of shock at the icy impact of that thunderous shower, then she found that Alain was right. It was fine once you got used to it. A marvellous feeling of exhilaration swept through her as she stood shuddering and laughing, watching great jets of water detonate against the rocks and ricochet into the pool below.

'It's fun, isn't it?' she shouted above the roar of the water.

'Can't hear you!' he yelled back.

She stood on tiptoe.

'Fun!' she bellowed.

And, as she did, she lost her footing on the slippery rocks, flailed wildly and lurched sideways. Alain's arms seemed to come from nowhere and he steadied her against him. Claire gasped breathlessly and clung to him, with her heart thudding. His body was cool and hard and rock-solid against her and she longed to remain there. For an instant she stayed still, tormenting herself with the fantasy that this was a real embrace, that Alain's arms were tightening about her so ruthlessly not merely to protect her, but to engulf her. Half blinded by the flying spray, she could not see the expression on his face, but for a second he seemed to be staring at her with stormy blue eyes, almost as if he intended to kiss her. Then she recovered her balance and edged away from him.

'T-thank you!' she gabbled, retreating back across the rocky floor of the pool. 'Look, shouldn't we be going now? It's really rather chilly in here, isn't it?'

He followed her in silence, his muscular body looming up out of the water with alarming vigour and a small, contemptuous smile playing about the corners of his mouth.

'I thought you hated meaningless small talk,' he reminded her as they reached dry ground.

She flinched at the hostility in his tone.

'Sorry,' she muttered.

'Don't bother apologising,' said Alain, clenching his fingers in her wet hair and jerking up her head so that she was forced to look at him. 'I've no real objection to your flirting with me, as you must have noticed. But what I really can't stand is the way you've brought the advance and retreat technique to a fine art. It's always one step forward and two steps back, isn't it, Claire? I think I'd prefer an outright invitation myself.'

Claire stared at him in horror.

'Flirting?' she echoed. 'Invitation? Oh, how can you?'

Her voice broke and she twisted her head away to hide the sudden rush of tears that were stinging her eyes. Alain's grip on her hair loosened fractionally, but he turned her ruthlessly back to face him.

'If I didn't know you better, I'd think that I had hurt you,' he murmured throatily.

Claire felt her pride slipping away from her and knew that tears were perilously close. So she took refuge in repartee.

'You have!' she retorted. 'In case you don't know it, you're pulling my hair!'

He released her at once and strode away, swearing softly under his breath. By the time she returned to the hut, he had already stripped off his bathing trunks and was towelling himself dry with angry, jerky movements, clearly quite indifferent as to whether she saw him naked or not. She waited until he was fully clothed and on his way to the car before she undressed herself. As she dried herself savagely with the towel, it was all she could do not to burst into tears.

The drive back home was spent in smouldering silence. Claire had assumed that he would take her straight home, but when they reached Point Cupid he turned into the hotel driveway.

'We'd better check whether there are any bookings for your inland tours tomorrow,' he said. 'Come inside with me and we'll ask the desk clerk.'

Sulkily Claire climbed out of the car and followed him into the cool, shady reception area. The moment Alain was inside the building, his surly manner vanished completely, and Claire would have been amused if she had not felt so aggrieved. It was rather impressive to see how Alain's staff snapped to attention the moment he came into sight and she had to give him credit for not inflicting his bad temper on his subordinates.

'Good morning, sir,' said a smiling doorman. 'Good morning, *mademoiselle*. The Paris papers have arrived, sir, and they're in your office if you want them.'

'Thank you, Edouard,' replied Alain pleasantly. 'And how's the new baby coming on?'

Edouard's smile widened even further.

'Very well, thank you, sir,' he said. 'My wife's going to write and thank you for the gift voucher.'

'My pleasure,' Alain assured him, guiding Claire across the lobby.

Everywhere they went Alain seemed to meet with the same warmth and respect. He must be a good employer, thought Claire shrewdly. It's obvious that people aren't just being pleasant because that's part of their job. There's real friendliness in the way they speak to him. Alain stopped at the tours desk and smiled at a middle-aged woman dressed in a blue pareu with a garland of flowers in her hair, who was talking on the telephone.

'One moment,' she mouthed.

As soon as she had hung up, she smiled at Alain.

'Good morning, sir,' she said. 'What can I do for you?'

'This is Mademoiselle Beaumont of Beaumont's Tours,' said Alain. 'We'd like to know if you have any bookings for the inland tours this week, Anne.'

'Yes, certainly,' agreed the clerk. 'And, *mademoiselle*, may I say that we were all very sorry to hear of your father's heart attack? Monsieur Beaumont is very well liked here.'

'Thank you,' said Claire sincerely, as she took the pile of booking forms from the other woman. 'I'll tell him that.'

'Oh, and *monsieur*,' added Catherine as Alain turned away, 'your housekeeper Paulette said that if you came in I should ask you whether you and the young lady would be eating lunch at your house. I believe she's cooked something special for you.'

'Claire?' prompted Alain. 'Will you be able to stay for lunch?'

Trapped, Claire stared at him in dismay. The last thing she wanted to do was spend an hour or more staring at him across a dining table, but it seemed ungracious to refuse. Particularly if Paulette had made something special.

'I...' she began. 'Well, that is... Yes, of course. Thank you. I'd be delighted.'

As they made their way back to the car, Alain smiled thinly.

'You're a hopeless liar,' he remarked, opening Claire's door and bundling her in. 'Delighted to have lunch with me, are you? I can't help feeling you'd look more delighted if you were attending your own funeral service.'

Claire scowled.

'Well, I didn't want to hurt Paulette's feelings,' she muttered. 'But I can't imagine why she made lunch for me in the first place.'

'Can't you?' drawled Alain, starting up the engine with a vicious twist of the keys. 'Well, I'll let you into the secret. I asked Paulette to make lunch for us on the offchance that you might want to stay. Of course, at that stage I thought we might be on friendly terms instead of at each other's throats.'

'Well, it's not my fault if we're at each other's throats,' retorted Claire heatedly.

'Isn't it?' sneered Alain. 'That's obviously a matter of opinion. But I assume you will at least be pleasant in front of Paulette so that she isn't upset by our differences?'

'Yes, I will,' hissed Claire with icy dignity.

When they reached Alain's house, Paulette was in the dining-room, putting the finishing touches to a beautifully arranged table near the huge window overlooking the sea. She turned around with a friendly smile as Alain ushered Claire into the room.

'Hello, Paulette,' said Claire, returning the smile. 'That looks lovely.'

She walked around the table, admiring the housekeeper's artistry. It was covered in a peach-coloured cloth and set with plain white plates of fine bone china, gleaming silver and Waterford crystal. In the centre was a lavish floral arrangement of frangipani, hibiscus and delicate spider ferns. Even the dishes of food were works of art. There were giant king prawns set in a circle on a huge platter garnished with wedges of lemon and sprigs of watercress, a lavish salad with the tomatoes cut into rosettes and a huge tropical trifle covered in

rosettes of cream and slices of golden pawpaw and green
Kiwi fruit.

'It's much too pretty to eat,' marvelled Claire.

Paulette beamed.

'Well, I hope you enjoy it, *mademoiselle*,' she said.
'Will there be anything else, sir?'

'No, thank you,' replied Alain. 'You can take the rest
of the afternoon off now.'

When Paulette had left, he picked up a bottle of chilled
white wine from a silver ice bucket and glanced enquir-
ingly at Claire.

'A glass of Riesling?' he suggested.

'Please.'

If she had not felt so conscious of the tension between
them, Claire would have enjoyed the lunch. The food
was delicious and Alain was an excellent host, casual
but attentive, with an easy flow of witty conversation.
But Claire could not get rid of the feeling that they were
both acting a part, circling around each other like a
couple of fencers, alert for the real struggle to begin.
Yet it was not until she had eaten her last delectable
mouthful of trifle and accepted Alain's offer of a liqueur
that the tension between them came to a head.

'Cointreau, did you say?' queried Alain.

'Yes, thank you.'

Their fingers touched as he passed her the glass of
clear, orange-scented liquid. Then he spoke in the same
low, pleasant voice he had used with the hotel staff.

'Did you find Marcel a satisfactory lover?' he asked.

It shocked Claire as badly as if he had slapped her
face. The glass jerked uncontrollably in her hand,
sending a jet of sticky fluid over her shorts. She caught
her breath and stared at him, her shoulders heaving.

'Stop it!' she choked.

'Why?' he demanded huskily.

Crouching down beside her so that his glittering blue
eyes were on a level with hers, he suddenly seized her

chin and stared at her with an angry, devouring
expression.

'I can't help thinking I could satisfy you at least as
deeply as Marcel,' he murmured. 'Do you think we
should give it a try?'

And to her horror and disbelief, he took her face between his hands and kissed her so violently that she let
out a whimper of protest. She struggled furiously, but
even as she struggled she was conscious of a deep, shuddering impulse to surrender. In a single, powerful
movement, Alain dragged her out of the chair and lifted
her off her feet, so that the entire length of her body
was pressed forcibly against him. She made a low sound
in the back of her throat and then her lips opened trem-
ulously against his. For an instant she gave herself up
to pure sensual abandonment, aware of nothing but his
wildly thudding heartbeat, the unendurably virile smell
of his body, the warm, intoxicating thrill of his kisses,
then some distant warning rang in her ears. Flattening
her palms against his chest, she tried feebly to push him
away.

'Put me down,' she whispered unsteadily.

He gave a harsh groan of laughter.

'Say that as if you mean it and I will,' he retorted.

His eyes were dark and narrowed with desire and there
was an intent, brooding savagery in his face.

'Well?' he taunted. 'Tell me that you really want me
to stop and I will.'

As he spoke, his grip tightened on her back, dragging
her against him so that she felt the warm, insistent
pressure of his manhood through the flimsy barrier of
their clothes. She wanted to protest, but their mouths
were locked greedily together, her eyelids were fluttering
shut and there was an insistent, pulsating warmth
spreading through her entire body. Time lost all meaning
as they stood there, but at last Alain set her down and
gripped her shoulders.

'Well?' he growled. 'Do you really want me to stop?'

Her eyes opened mistily and she looked up at him, dazed with love and yearning. Wordlessly she shook her head. Alain gave a low, exultant laugh and swept her off her feet. In a few swift strides, he was out of the room and striding down the hall. When he reached the bedroom, he flung her down on the bed, stripped off her sandals and hurled them across the room. His own shoes followed suit, then he knelt above her, devouring her with his eyes.

'Do you know that I've wanted you from the first moment I saw you?' he demanded hoarsely.

'In the airport?' she faltered, tracing the outline of his jaw with one tentative finger.

A shudder went through his entire body.

'No. Earlier, much earlier,' he muttered, half to himself. 'But you were too young, only a girl. It wouldn't have been right. But now you're all woman, aren't you, Claire? Ripe and beautiful and ready for a man to possess you?'

A strange ache spread through Claire's limbs at these words. She loved Alain so desperately that it was all she could do not to gasp out her feelings in an incoherent babble of emotion. Instead she reached up and locked her hands around his neck, drawing his head down to hers.

'Yes,' she breathed.

Her lips parted softly and she brushed her open mouth against his. With a strangled moan, he seized her by the head and kissed her with a violence that both terrified and exalted her. Then he sat back on his heels, and slowly and deliberately began unbuttoning her blouse. Feasting his eyes on her emerging nakedness, he drew her up into a sitting position and slid the garment off her shoulders.

'I want to kiss every inch of you,' he growled.

With merciless fingers, he unfastened her bra and flung it away. Her large, pink-tipped breasts swung free and

he cupped them in his hands and caressed them
provocatively.

'Now I want to taste you,' he murmured hoarsely and,
pushing her back on to the pillows, he bent his head and
tugged her nipple gently with his teeth.

She gasped at the tingling warmth of that sensual,
biting caress. Bewildered by the urgent sensations that
were pulsing through her, she tried to struggle up, but
found herself pushed ruthlessly back.

'All in good time,' he murmured. 'You'll have your
chance, believe me. But for the moment I'm going to
do exactly what I want with you, Claire. And what I
want is to take you in my mouth and tease you until I
feel your nipples go hard and hear you begin to gasp
and call my name. Oh, yes, like that, my darling. Just
like that.'

'Alain!' she choked. 'Oh, Alain, please, I can't bear
it...it's too...oh, yes, yes, yes.'

For now her nipples had risen into hard, urgent peaks
and his warm mouth was straying further down her body,
leaving a trail of fire on her skin. Nuzzling her silken
belly, he let out a low chuckle.

'What is it?' she asked.

'You taste all sweet and sticky and fiery,' he explained.

'I-it's the Cointreau,' she stammered. 'I'll wash it off.'

'No!' His upraised arm barred her way like a steel
barrier. 'Let me lick it off for you.'

The pungent, sweet liqueur had dried to form a sticky
crust on her skin and at the first touch of Alain's tongue
she squirmed and giggled protestingly. But the truth was
that those warm, moist, caressing strokes were unbearably erotic, feathering over her skin until excitement seemed to blaze like wildfire in every cell of
her body. When Alain's merciless fingers sought the
waistband of her shorts, she did not protest. And when
he peeled away the final barrier of her silk knickers, she
lay on one elbow, watching him out of sultry, half-closed

eyes, aware that the banked fires of passion were soon going to rage totally out of control. Burying his face in her smooth belly, Alain made a low sound deep in the back of his throat and nuzzled her skin with his face. The slight rasping of his chin against her satiny body made her quiver with arousal.

'Your turn now,' ordered Alain.

And, taking her slim fingers in a merciless grip, he guided them to the buttons of his shirt.

'Undress me,' he said curtly.

Her hands trembled as she hauled the shirt over his head. But when his lean, muscular torso was revealed, she forgot all about being shy and yielded to the impulse to slide her fingers over the dark, springy hair that grew there. Alain took her right hand in his, kissed each fingertip slowly and then guided it down to the top of his shorts.

'If you want to stop, tell me now,' he warned in a hoarse undertone. 'There'll be no going back after this.'

'I know,' she whispered, aware only that wave after wave of fire seemed to be throbbing through her body.

Leaning sensually forward, she kissed Alain with her lips open and inviting. Her breasts brushed against his naked chest and he caught his breath sharply. His grip on her hand tightened and he thrust it ruthlessly down.

'Touch me,' he urged. 'Hold me.'

At her first tentative caress, pure madness seemed to overtake them both. With urgent, frenzied movements Alain stripped off his shorts and flung them aside, then hauled her down on top of him. The feel of his naked, virile body with its steely muscles and rough, springy hair awoke a deep, primitive response in Claire. Her body throbbed and blazed with heat and her eyes felt misty and strange with desire. Thought and reason were temporarily suspended and there was only an insistent, savage hunger that demanded satisfaction. The room whirled about her in a dizzy panorama as Alain rolled wildly with her and fetched up on top of her, crushing her beneath his powerful frame.

'Kiss me,' he growled, threading his fingers through her hair and jerking up her head.

She obeyed, opening her mouth but tormenting him deliberately with small, nibbling kisses that left him unsatisfied.

'Oh, would you now?' he murmured hoarsely and, seizing her chin, he held her forcibly in place and took his revenge.

His lips were warm and fierce and his tongue probed the sweet crevices of her mouth in a totally ruthless fashion. Yet somehow his ruthlessness made it doubly exciting. Seizing her arms, he pinioned her wrists and loomed over her like an arrogant conqueror.

'Do you give in?' he demanded.

Impishly she shook her head.

'Not yet,' she purred teasingly and showed him the tip of her tongue.

He made a low sound in the back of his throat and buried his face in the hollow of her throat, lowering his full weight on top of her again so that he crushed her beneath him. His breath tickled her ear, sending quivering thrills of excitement through her entire body.

'You will, my love. You will,' he threatened. 'By the time I've finished with you, you'll surrender to me totally. I want everything you've got to give, do you understand me? Everything. And I intend to take it too.'

That low, smoky, vibrant baritone sent thrills of excitement coursing up and down Claire's spine and she wriggled involuntarily. The movement brought their bodies into even closer contact and she felt the hard, insistent stirring of his manhood against her.

'Is that a promise?' she breathed into his ear.

'You sensual little...' he swore softly. 'I'm going to teach you a thing or two and that is a promise. Starting with this.'

Claire had never known that such pure, distilled ecstasy could exist. Alain's hands and mouth were maddeningly skilful and he had no inhibitions whatsoever about using them. Again and again he brought her to the point of whimpering and totally blissful loss of control before he took his final revenge. Only when she was writhing and twisting in his hold, uttering small, gasping cries and arching her body instinctively against him, did he bring their encounter to its rightful conclusion.

'Well, are you all mine?' he whispered hoarsely into her ear.

'Yes... Yes!' she shuddered.

'Will you let me do whatever I choose with you?'

'Mmmm...mmm...'

They were no more than disjointed gasps, but by now she was almost beyond coherent speech.

'Alain...please,' she begged.

A triumphant smile lit his eyes and curled the corners of his sardonic lips. But his hands did not cease their merciless, tantalising torment.

'So you're my woman, are you, Claire?' he insisted. 'Mine totally and completely?'

'Yes,' she gasped.

'Good,' he replied. And drove into her.

Claire's body arched to meet him and she gloried in his fierce, male vigour. He was all taut muscle and invincible power and a proud, shameless joy pulsed through her at every forceful thrust. For a long time there was no sound in the room but their low, inarticulate cries, the shallow, fast rhythm of their breathing and the protesting creak of the bed springs. Claire closed her eyes, drowning in the ecstatic sensations that were building with ominous force inside her. Her fingers were tangled in Alain's thick, wavy hair, she felt the satisfying hardness of his full weight upon her and smelt the primitive odour of a fully aroused male. A tremor went through her as she felt the first, uncertain signs of approaching fulfilment. Her head threshed wildly from side to side and her body tensed like a fully drawn bow.

'Alain,' she muttered. 'Alain ... I ... oh, oh, oh.'

Like a hang glider launching into space, she soared over some invisible edge and reached a climax that overpowered her. Gasping and shuddering, she thrust herself at Alain, digging her fingers convulsively into his back and crying his name. Her eyes fluttered open and she saw him gazing down at her, his face dark and contorted with desire. He said nothing, but with a sudden violent spasm he clutched her more urgently against him as he reached his own peak.

They lay for a long time, spent and shuddering, too overpowered to move. Claire felt exhausted but utterly transfigured, and she was glad that Alain did not slide off her. It was pure joy to feel the crushing weight of his body, warm and heavy and slick with sweat, to hold him against her and know that he was hers. Gradually her heartbeat slowed to normal and she became aware of a pleasant, drowsy ache that filled her loins. There was no doubt that Alain was a magnificent lover, but there was more to it than that. It was not just his undoubted skill in bed that left her breathless. It was the sense of complete and utter union that she had found in his arms. A wave of emotion surged through her at the thought and she hugged him hard against her.

'I love you, Alain,' she whispered. 'I love you so much.'

His head came up at that and his blue eyes blazed at her, narrow and cruel and suspicious.

'There's no need to say that,' he said in a hard voice. 'You don't have to pretend, Claire. It was just a casual fling for both of us, so why say any different?'

She stared at him in horror, as he drew himself away from her and rose to his feet.

'Don't say that, Alain!' she cried. 'It's not true, not for me, anyway. I do love you! I wouldn't have done it otherwise.'

He was silent for several seconds, hauling on his clothes with restless, angry movements.

'Look, Claire,' he snapped at last. 'I can just about cope with the idea that you're a sensual woman who enjoys sex and makes no bones about it. But this pretence that I'm the one and only man you love really sticks in my throat. So do me a favour and stop it, will you?'

Her eyes filled with tears.

'You bastard!' she wailed. 'You arrogant, exploitative bastard! Do you mean to tell me you made love to me just for a bit of cheap, quick sexual satisfaction? And then you have the gall to pretend that that's all I want too? Well, let me tell you——'

But what was she going to tell him, Alain never found out, for at that moment the front doorbell rang. Throwing him a look filled with hatred, Claire scrambled out of bed and began to collect her scattered clothes. Alain's grip closed on her wrist like a steel bracelet.

'What do you think you're doing?' he demanded.

'I'm leaving!' she spat at him. 'There's not much point sticking around now that we've both had our satisfaction, is there?'

The doorbell rang again imperiously.

'Claire, wait!' ordered Alain with an expression like thunder. 'There are things we've got to discuss!'

She twisted away from him, tossing her head defiantly.

'Please!' he added angrily.

The absurdity of pleading in such a tone struck her even at this unlikely moment and her lips quirked. She hesitated. He drew her against him and his lips brushed the top of her hair.

'I'll have to go,' he muttered reluctantly. 'There may be some emergency at the hotel. But I'll be back. Wait for me?'

She paused, watching the muscle twitching at his temple, the brooding look in his eyes. Then she let out her breath in a long sigh and nodded.

The door closed behind him and Claire picked up the rest of her clothes and began to dress. Her emotions were in utter turmoil and her legs seemed to be shaking so much that they would hardly hold her. What was going on? What did Alain mean? What were his real feelings towards her? Did he really think she had only made love with him out of pure and simple lust? And was that all he felt towards her? At the thought a small, dry sob escaped her. Her fingers trembled as she sat down to buckle her sandals. No. There was some reasonable explanation, some meaning to his harsh words. There must be. As soon as he had sorted out the caller at the door, she would ask him about it. In fact, the person might already have left.

Turning the handle, she opened the door quietly and stepped into the hall. But as she neared the sitting-room, it became obvious that the caller hadn't left at all. Two voices were raised in heated debate. One was Alain's, calm and infuriatingly reasonable. The other was Nadine's. Angry, reproachful and very, very loud.

'What the hell do you mean, you had to spend the day sorting out Claire Beaumont's affairs? What sort of claim has she got on you, I'd like to know? Anyway, have you forgotten that you were supposed to be flying to Bora Bora with me today?'

CHAPTER SEVEN

CLAIRE felt icy with shock at these words. The rapid unfolding of events since the wedding had driven all thoughts of Alain's planned trip to Bora Bora out of her mind. In fact, only now did she realise that it actually was Monday. She waited with a terrible sense of misgiving for Alain to say something, to offer an explanation that would soothe all her uneasiness. But Alain's next words were hardly reassuring.

'Don't be ridiculous, Nadine,' he said sharply. 'Of course I hadn't forgotten. And nothing important has changed about my plans to stay there with you. Didn't you get my message from the front desk, telling you to fly ahead without me?'

'Yes,' muttered Nadine resentfully. 'But it didn't explain anything.'

Alain clicked his tongue.

'What is there to explain?' he demanded. 'I was unavoidably detained with Claire Beaumont, but I fully intended to fly over and join you tomorrow. All that has happened is that my plans have been set back by one day, but I've every intention of spending a week on Bora Bora with you, exactly as we planned. So for heaven's sake, stop fussing.'

Claire's heart almost stopped at this brazen announcement. How dared he? she thought. How dared he? So I'm just a trivial interlude before the big event with Nadine, am I? Oh, I could kill him! Biting her lips against the sob that was rising in her throat, she backed silently away down the corridor. As she reached the back of the house, the storm of weeping broke and her eyes were blurred with tears as she fumbled her way out of the laundry door and sprinted towards her car.

'Swine, swine, swine!' she breathed, pounding her fists on the steering-wheel and sobbing helplessly. 'Oh, God, I hope I never have to see you again in my life!'

Yet reason told her that Alain would not give up easily. Whatever cock-eyed view of love made him want to have affairs with two women at once would undoubtedly send him in pursuit of her and she would have to be prepared to confront him, however much she hated the thought. She wept all the way home and throughout the half-hour that she spent in a lukewarm bath, scrubbing every trace of her encounter with Alain off her body. But by four o'clock she had cried herself to a standstill and knew that if she was ever going to hold her head up again she would have to hit back. Splashing her face with cold water, she found her make-up bag, prowled angrily into her room and began hauling her smartest dresses off their hangers and throwing them on her bed. Within half an hour she was clad in a crisp pale blue and white striped frock. Her hair was drawn back into a rather severe chignon, her lips were highlighted with coral gloss and her eyes looked larger and darker than ever with a discreet brown eyeshadow. She was confident that she looked cool and businesslike. Yet, even so, her heart skipped uncomfortably when the doorbell rang. The outline of a tall, powerful body through the frosted glass sent a tremor of apprehension through her.

'Hello, Alain,' she murmured with a faint, superior smile, as she opened the door. 'What can I do for you?'

'Don't give me that patronising rubbish,' he snarled, striding into the sitting-room without waiting to be asked. 'Why the hell did you go off like that?'

He did not look as suave and self-assured as usual. His navy shorts and white polo shirt were well cut and expensive looking, but his dark hair was wildly disordered as if he had been running his fingers through it and there were dangerous spots of colour high on his cheekbones. An aura of angry, forceful vitality radiated out from his entire body, so that he seemed to take possession of the entire room.

'Well? Answer me!' he snapped.

Claire bristled. His appearance had taken her aback, but now resentment came surging to her aid, hot and heady. She shrugged charmingly.

'There didn't seem to be much point in staying around once the action was over,' she replied coolly.

Sparks flashed in his eyes. His voice, when it came, was throaty and almost menacing.

'This afternoon you told me that you loved me,' he said. 'What did you mean by that?'

Claire gave a small, rippling laugh and fluttered her eyelashes at him.

'Well, it's the sort of thing one says in those circumstances, isn't it?' she replied teasingly. 'After all, it adds to the atmosphere, doesn't it? Provided one doesn't take it too seriously.'

Alain swore under his breath.

'Oh, don't worry, sweetheart,' he sneered. 'I'm hardly likely to make the mistake of taking you seriously, knowing you as I do. But life doesn't have to be all serious, does it? I'm going to Bora Bora tomorrow on business for a week, but there's all the time in the world when I come back. What would you say to dinner and a nightclub?'

'A nightclub?' drawled Claire.

Alain's hand moved towards her with hypnotic slowness. His fingers caressed her cheek and moved tantalisingly down the hollow of her throat until they touched her left breast. For a moment she stood, unable to move, unable even to breath. Slowly and deliberately he traced a whorl of fire on her nipple. Claire shuddered and, with an effort of will, stepped back.

'Yes, a nightclub,' mused Alain, watching the colour surge into her face. 'Or perhaps a late-night game of tennis with a little re-match afterwards?'

Claire recovered her poise.

'How sweet of you to suggest it, Alain,' she purred. 'But I'm likely to be very busy next week. Danny Abbott is having another stop-over in Tahiti on his way back from the United States.'

Alain caught his breath.

'Are you telling me that you're going to sleep with him again?' he asked in a dangerous voice.

Claire smiled enigmatically.

'I'm not telling you anything,' she retorted. 'I think it's awfully bad taste to tell tales about one's sex life.'

Alain's fingers clenched furiously on her shoulders and his blue eyes scorched into hers. To her horror, Claire found his tense, contained anger deeply arousing, and she had to resist the urge to burrow into his arms. Either that or pound on his chest with clenched fists and shout her grievances at him. But she knew that either of those courses could only have one possible end. If she let herself soften even a fraction towards him, he would make love to her with a passion that would shake her to the core. And, however much her body might yearn for his touch, she was not prepared to share him with Nadine. Drawing a long, shaky breath, she folded her arms and smiled superciliously.

'You little slut!' he breathed.

Breaking away from her, he strode across the room. His hands clenched into fists of rage, but he controlled himself with obvious effort.

'All right, Claire,' he snarled, turning back to face her. 'You've made it perfectly plain that our encounter was nothing more than an idle frolic as far as you're concerned. Well, I wish to God I'd never laid hands on you, but you have my promise that it won't happen again. Don't bother coming with me. I'll see myself out!'

Moments later the front door slammed with a force that set the pictures swinging on the wall. Claire collapsed slowly into a chair and rocked herself backwards and forwards, with low, gasping cries. Pain seared through her with scalding force and, try as she might, she could not feel any pleasure in her victory. She had taken her revenge on Alain, just as she'd intended. So why did she feel so wretched?

The next three weeks were a difficult time for Claire. Somehow she seemed to be encased in a cocoon of misery, where the only thing she could feel was the pain of her feud with Alain. Her body went through the motions of everyday life, getting up, eating, running the tours, visiting her father in hospital, but she felt detached from it all. To try and raise her spirits, she took up *tamure* dancing again and joined a local troupe which was practising for the big July festival. Yet her heart wasn't in it. At night she slept badly, suffering vivid nightmares where she argued and pleaded with Alain, or, worse still, made love with him. But in the mornings she always woke to find herself alone with her bed in total chaos and her cheeks crusted with tears. Fortunately the tour business was booming and she found herself committed to doing two or even three tours per day, seven days a week. It was exhausting, but Claire welcomed the work, because it gave her less time to think about Alain. And it also gave her the opportunity to save some money to pay off her father's debt, since she was grimly determined that the Beaumont's must owe Alain nothing.

After two weeks, she had enough money set aside to send him a substantial cheque as the first instalment. He sent it back, without any covering letter. Fuming, Claire sent it to him yet again. This time he kept it, but did not cash it. Claire had to admit defeat. And the worst of it was that she realised she had been secretly hoping for some contact with Alain over the issue. A letter, a quarrelsome telephone call, an angry visit. In the end she swallowed her pride enough to phone the hotel and ask for him. But his secretary told her that he had returned to Bora Bora and was staying there indefinitely. And she added apologetically that he was not taking any personal calls.

This stalemate continued until the third week after their heated parting, when something happened to shake Claire out of her lethargy. Marie Rose returned from her honeymoon. Because of her father's illness, it was agreed that she should stay overnight in Papeete to visit him in hospital and rejoin her husband on Moorea the following day. But once Marie Rose had satisfied herself about Roland's state of health, she turned her attention relentlessly to Claire. Throughout the hospital visit, Claire was conscious of her sister darting her speculative looks and, when they reached home, Marie Rose lost no time in asking questions.

'What's the matter with you, Claire?' she demanded, as they began preparing dinner. 'You look pale and bug-eyed and awful. Are you sick or something?'

With this sisterly encouragement, Claire took a long, choking gulp, snatched a handful of tissues and blew her nose violently. Once she was able to talk again, Marie Rose patiently extracted all the relevant details from her, while simultaneously stirring a large pot of *boeuf bourguignon*. Her questions were so shrewd and penetrating that in the end Claire broke down and confessed everything to her, right down to her involvement with Marcel Sauvage. Marie Rose gave a low whistle of shock.

'No wonder Alain took so long to get involved with you,' she said. 'It seems to me that you both have a big problem with trusting each other.'

Claire's eyes blazed indignantly.

'Alain is the one with the problem!' she protested. 'Not me!'

'Well, you certainly didn't make things any easier for him, did you?' demanded Marie Rose. 'Lying to him like that about how you were having an affair with poor old Danny Abbott! What on earth possessed you, Claire?'

'I didn't lie!' said Claire sulkily. 'Alain simply jumped to conclusions.'

'Lying,' insisted Marie Rose. 'You deliberately deceived him.'

'It was his own fault,' muttered Claire. 'He didn't have any scruples about sleeping with Nadine when he was already involved with me, did he?'

'I still can't believe that Alain made love to you and then went off to Bora Bora for a holiday with Nadine the very next day!' exclaimed Marie Rose. 'It's impossible.'

'It's true!' wailed Claire.

'We'll soon see about that!' announced Marie Rose with a militant light in her eyes. 'Listen, Claire, Paul and I have to go and visit Alain anyway to check on some details about the blueprints for the Moorea hotel. Do you want me to find out what's really going on between him and Nadine?'

Claire hesitated. She was sorely tempted by the prospect of having a spy in the enemy's camp, but pride made her toss her head.

'No!' she sniffed. 'Why should I care what's going on between him and Nadine? It doesn't matter to me.'

'Oh, don't be silly,' said Marie Rose tranquilly, dipping her finger into the wooden spoon and licking off a morsel of stew. 'You can't fool me. I'll telephone you tomorrow night and tell you everything. I promise.'

Throughout the next day Claire found her mind wandering as she steered the four-wheel-drive car over rugged mountain tracks and down precipitous, leafy hillsides. However much she might try to pretend that she hated Alain, some part of her brain still clung to the hope that their vendetta was all a mistake. Deep down she was secretly convinced that Marie Rose, with her bloodhound instincts, would uncover some evidence that Alain was innocent. Some proof that he had only gone to Bora Bora with Nadine to examine drainage systems or Polynesian architecture, perhaps? And, when at last the phone rang shortly after eight o'clock, her hands were shaking as she picked up the receiver.

'Marie Rose?'

The long pause at the other end of the line made her spirits plummet.

'Yes, it's me,' said Marie Rose at last, with none of her usual bounce.

Even then Claire could not quite give up hope.

'W-well?' she asked with a valiant attempt at humour. 'Are they just investigating damp courses or doing a survey of Polynesian unemployment?'

'In a way,' agreed Marie Rose heavily. 'Alain's talking about building a new hotel there and he's asked Nadine to draw some preliminary plans, but——'

'But?' urged Claire.

'But they're definitely sleeping together,' continued Marie Rose. 'We went to visit them in the holiday bungalow they were staying at. There was only one bedroom and their clothes were in the same wardrobe. I know because I went in to use the bathroom and I checked.'

'Oh,' said Claire in a small voice, feeling as if a knife had gone into her heart. 'Well, that's it then, isn't it?'

Two large tears sprang to her eyes, slid down her cheeks and splashed on her lap.

'Are you all right, Claire?' asked Marie Rose anxiously.

'Me? Oh, yes. Fine. Never been better. Look, I must go. I've got coffee boiling over on the stove. Or something.'

'I'm so sorry, Claire. I never would have believed it of Alain. How could he be so heartless?'

Those words echoed over and over in Claire's head that night as she lay awake, watching the shadows of the banana fronds stir against her moonlit wall. Outside a faint breeze rustled the trees and the waves whispered on the sand. The lagoon was like a vast sheet of beaten silver and the warm scented aromas of a tropical night blew in through the open window. But all that tranquillity meant nothing to Claire. She lay in stark, tearless agony, her fists clenched and her eyes wide open, as she relived her tempestuous lovemaking with Alain. Once again she felt the intoxicating pressure of his body on hers, saw the urgent blaze in his eyes that told her he loved her, even if the words were lacking. With a low groan, she turned her face into the pillow. She hadn't imagined it, she knew she hadn't! At least in those moments when they had shared the ultimate ecstasy, Alain had loved her. Then how could he turn so blithely from her to Nadine? How *could* he be so heartless?

In the end she fell into a troubled doze, but she woke shortly after eight o'clock with a headache and sore eyes. While she was gulping down her coffee in frantic haste, the telephone rang. No longer expecting any miracles, she answered it and found that it was her mother, phoning to say that her father would be discharged from hospital the following day. Claire felt barely a flicker of excitement at the news, but she tried to inject some warmth into her voice.

'That's wonderful, Maman!' she said. 'What time shall I come and fetch you both?'

To Claire's dismay, she found that her parents' return the following day only seemed to compound her problems. Naturally she was glad that her father was recovering, but her mother showed an irritating urge to question her about her listless manner and poor appetite. And, after several years of living in her own flat,

Claire found that constant daily contact with her parents chafed her nerves. There were times when she longed to go back on her word, give up the tour business and flee to her job in Sydney. But that would mean throwing her family on Alain's mercy, which was unthinkable. In the end all she could do was grit her teeth and spend as much time as possible out on the road, working. Which was what finally led to disaster.

One afternoon Claire received a phone call at her home, asking her to take two people on the Mount Marau tour. She hesitated, looking doubtfully out the window at the flying buttresses of cloud that were massing overhead.

'I'm sorry,' she said. 'I don't really think it would be a good idea. I normally leave much earlier in the day for that particular trip and it looks rather like rain to me this afternoon. The roads up there can be quite dangerous when they're wet. What about tomorrow morning instead?'

'Oh, come on, mate,' wheedled the voice at the other end. 'The forecast's for fine weather today and we're flying out to Los Angeles tomorrow. Tell you what, we'll pay you double if you'll take us.'

'Oh, I couldn't do that,' replied Claire hastily. 'It's not the money I'm worried about. It's your safely.'

'Well, what about giving it a go? If it starts to rain, you can turn around and come back. Fair enough?'

Claire sighed.

'All right,' she agreed.

Her passengers proved to be two red-faced, strapping young Australian men full of jokes and boisterous laughter. As they climbed aboard, one of them flexed a massive bicep at her.

'Don't worry, love,' he grinned. 'If you get bogged, me and Wayne'll push you out again.'

In spite of that reassurance, Claire kept an uneasy eye on the sky as she drove out of town. The sun had vanished and vast grey banks of cloud were massing in the sky. Far down below the ocean glittered with a dull metallic gleam like pewter and the air was heavy with an ominous stillness. As they reached the first of the Chinese market gardens, there was a distant rumble of thunder and the first large drops of rain ricocheted off the bonnet of the car.

'I think we ought to go back,' she said in a worried voice.

The red-headed youth called Bruce leaned forward over the seat and winked at her in the rear-view mirror.

'Oh, go a bit further, love,' he urged. 'We don't mind a drop of rain. Anyway, maybe she'll ease up in a minute.'

But the rain didn't ease up. Soon it was falling in steady sheets and the roar of wind and thunder filled the air. In the glare of a sudden flash of lightning Claire saw the road ahead change from tarmac to slick red mud.

'It's hopeless!' she shouted above the noise of the storm. 'I'll have to turn and go home.'

Even the optimists in the back seat were forced to agree with that.

'Yeah, reckon you're right, mate,' agreed Wayne. 'Sorry we brought you out for nothing. Hey, what are you doing?'

For Claire had stopped the car and was turning up the collar of her jacket.

'I'll have to get out and engage the four-wheel-drive,' she said. 'I don't think I can turn safely without getting the wheels in the mud and they'll never grip in this weather.'

'Course you can,' urged Bruce heartily. 'You've got heaps of room before the dirt road starts. But if you've really got the wind up, I'll get out and change to four-wheel-drive for you.'

'Oh, no, don't worry!' begged Claire. 'I'm sure you're right. I'm sure I can turn it on the bitumen quite safely. It's just that——'

Hauling on the wheel, she brought the vehicle nosing around in a cautious arc. Ahead of her rain came sheeting down, making the edge of the road totally invisible. Her heart thudded wildly as she wondered whether she was coming too close to that terrifying drop, but the car seemed to be responding magnificently. For one triumphant moment Claire thought she had done it, then the back wheels hit the dirt road. The car spun totally out of control, poised lazily on the brink of the precipice and, with a sickening jolt, hurtled straight over the edge.

'Alain!' screamed Claire.

Wet trees rushed up to meet them, there was a confused impression of rain and darkness and her head hit something with violent force...

'She's coming round, mate,' said a deep voice. 'Here, give us that wet cloth.'

A cold, damp sensation descended on her aching forehead.

'Alain...Alain,' she whimpered.

'Are you feeling better now, love?'

Wincing, she opened her eyes. What she actually felt was a dizzy, nauseating urge to be sick. But as she saw the gloomy interior of the car and heard the roar of the rain outside, memory came hurtling back. Fortunately a tree seemed to have broken their fall, although the vehicle was leaning drunkenly to one side and the front windscreen was shattered. But what about her passengers? Had she killed either of them?

'Are you both all right?' she demanded sharply. 'Did you get hurt?'

'Nah. Reckon our skulls were too thick to suffer any damage,' replied Wayne with a chuckle. 'You gave us a bit of a turn, though. Thought you were a goner for a minute there. Listen, mate, tell them she's come round now.'

The last words were addressed to Bruce. Blinking owlishly, Claire saw that she had been laid out on her side in the back seat of the car with a rug over her. In the front seat Bruce was talking into the two-way radio, speaking slowly and clearly above the static from the storm.

'They want to know if you can move everything,' he said to Claire.

Experimentally she wiggled her toes and stretched her arms.

'Yes,' she replied.

'Yeah, she can. All right. Over and out.' He leaned over the seat and grinned cheerfully at her. 'Don't worry, love. Some bloke called Alain is coming up to get us right away.'

Alain! Claire closed her eyes and groaned. That was all she needed—to have Alain come and see what a mess she had made of everything. Running off the road, nearly killing two tourists, wrecking her father's tour vehicle. No doubt he would scorch the hide off her with his sarcasm when he arrived.

Yet, when Alain finally did arrive, he showed no inclination whatever to be sarcastic. The first sign of his arrival was a loud hail from the road twenty feet above. Bruce immediately scrambled out of the car, cupped his hands and shouted back. Moments later a figure in a yellow rain slicker came hurrying down the bank, wrenched open the car door and loomed over Claire.

'Are you really all right?' demanded Alain hoarsely, seizing her hands.

'Yes,' she choked.

He held her against his shiny, wet raincoat for an instant and hugged her tightly. Then he became brisk and practical.

'What about you fellows?' he asked the two Australians. 'Any injuries?'

'No, mate, we're fine,' Wayne assured him.

'Just the same, I'd like you to have a medical check up in Papeete. Go to whichever doctor your hotel recommends and tell him to send me the bill. Alain Charpentier is the name. They're sure to know it. Now let's get you all out of here.'

Lifting Claire in his arms, Alain carried her up the bank as easily as if there were no steep, muddy slope, no tangling vines and no torrential rain to impede his progress. He was not even breathing heavily when he set her down by the roadside. Through the driving rain Claire saw the headlights of two stationary vehicles. Alain opened the door of one of them and helped her inside. Then he turned to address the two young men who had just reached the edge of the road. Winding down the window, Claire heard his words.

'One of my employees is in the other car. He'll drive you back to your hotel and give you a refund on your tour tickets. And if you'd like to have dinner at the Hotel Miharo at Point Cupid tonight, it will be on the house.'

'Look, mate,' protested Bruce, 'you don't have to do that.'

'I insist,' said Alain. 'Claire, wind up that window before you get wet through.'

Ignoring this command, Claire put her hand out and touched Bruce's sleeve.

'I'm awfully sorry about the accident,' she said.

'Don't say that,' he replied uncomfortably. 'I reckon we're the ones who ought to be apologising. It was mainly our fault.'

Both young men shook hands with her and then climbed into the other car. Alain stood by with folded arms and only when they had driven away did he climb in beside Claire.

'What the hell did he mean by that?' he demanded.

Nervously Claire stammered out an explanation of all that had happened. Alain swore under his breath.

'You little fool.' he snarled. 'Don't you realise you could have killed yourself? Well, that's the last time you ever drive that car on an inland tour again. I forbid it! Do you hear me?'

'Who are you to forbid——?' began Claire hotly and then subsided.

A jag of pain shot through her bruised forehead and she thought of the shattered windscreen and smashed bonnet of the mangled vehicle.

'Come to think of it, I don't suppose anybody will be driving it again,' she admitted unsteadily. 'I really wrecked it, didn't I? All Papa's work down the drain!'

'All your work down the drain, you mean,' contradicted Alain. 'You know damned well your father very rarely worked more than four hours a day, but from what Eve tells me you've been running yourself into the ground. What were you trying to do? Kill yourself?'

Claire winced.

'Don't shout at me!' she protested.

With an effort Alain controlled himself. His right hand came out and gripped her knee briefly.

'I'm sorry,' he said in a surly tone. 'You damned near scared the life out of me with what you did. But don't worry too much about the vehicle. Even if it is too badly wrecked to be repaired, the insurance will cover it.'

Ahead of them the street-lights of Papeete gleamed luridly through the rain. Claire closed her eyes, listening to the hiss of the tyres on the wet road, the surge and rush of the windscreen wipers, the faint sound of Alain's breathing. Absurdly, however much she hated him, it seemed amazingly comforting simply to drift and let him take care of everything. Her head slipped sideways and she dozed.

'Are you all right, Claire?'

  She jolted awake to find herself still in the car in front
of Alain's house. The rain had stopped and the evening
air was filled with the fragarance of a moist, tropical
garden.

  'What am I doing here?' she mumbled. 'Why didn't
you take me home?'

  Alain seized her hand and hauled her ruthlessly out
of the car.

  'In the first place because I want the hotel doctor to
examine you,' he explained. 'And in the second place,
because I think you should tidy up before you see your
father. You'd probably scare him into a second heart
attack at the moment.'

  Following Alain into the entrance hall, Claire caught
sight of herself in a mirror and realised that he was right.
Her hair was plastered to her scalp with rain and mud,
her clothes were filthy, her face was deathly pale and
there was a large lump on the left side of her forehead.

  'Go into my bedroom, take a shower and get into bed,'
ordered Alain. 'There should be a towelling robe on the
back of the door that you can put on. I'll phone the
doctor.'

  It was heavenly to strip off her filthy, sodden clothes
and stand under the thunderous downpour of the shower.
Her head still ached and there were some tender spots
on her breasts and left shoulder where the seat belt had
cut into her skin, but she felt better than she expected.
In fact a giddy, almost drunken hilarity seemed to have
overtaken her, so that she sang as she shampooed her
hair. When she had towelled herself dry, she pulled on
Alain's bathrobe, tied another towel in a turban round
her head and went into the bedroom. Apart from the
fact that her legs trembled slightly, she felt fine.

  She had barely climbed into bed when there was a brisk
knock at the door and the hotel doctor appeared. He
was a small, balding man with twinkling grey eyes, spec-
tacles and tufts of hair like steel wool over his ears.

'Well, well, how are we feeling now?' he asked cheerfully, setting down his bag, taking out his stethoscope and feeling Claire's pulse without a moment's pause.

Five minutes later, he called Alain in to join them.

'Fit as a flea,' he announced with satisfaction. 'Bit of a bump on the forehead and some minor bruises, but nothing serious. The only danger now would be if she suffers from delayed shock. Best thing you can do to avoid that is keep her warm and in bed, give her a light meal and see that she gets a good night's sleep.'

'I'll do that,' promised Alain, as he escorted the doctor to the door.

Claire lay back with her eyes closed, enjoying the luxurious feeling of crisp, lavender-scented sheets, a light thermal blanket and deep feather pillows. The fact that she hated Alain and never wanted to see him again seemed curiously remote as she drifted between sleeping and waking in the darkened room. Some time later there were firm masculine footsteps beside the bed and a lamp was switched on, bathing the room in a soft apricot glow.

'Come in now, Paulette,' ordered Alain.

His beaming housekeeper tiptoed into the room with a tray. Claire sat up and found herself looking at a steaming ham and mushroom omelette, a tossed green salad, a crisp roll and butter and a bowl of *crème caramel*. Deftly Alain piled the pillows behind her and handed her a glass of apple juice.

'I've phoned your parents and told them you're well, but that you're staying here tonight in case of delayed shock,' he said.

'Oh, but that's absurd,' protested Claire. 'I can perfectly well——'

'How on earth do you think your mother will cope if you're taken ill during the night?' he cut in. 'Don't you think she's been through enough lately?'

Claire bit her lip and subsided.

'Now eat your supper,' said Alain in a kinder tone. 'There's no need to wait for the tray, Paulette. I'll collect it when Claire has finished and you can clean up properly when you come in the morning.'

'Whatever you say sir,' agreed Paulette. 'I hope you're better soon, *mademoiselle*.'

'Thank you,' murmured Claire with a smile.

Left alone, she made a good meal. The omelette was crisp and savoury, the salad dressing had a tang of lemon and basil and the *crème caramel* slid smoothly and sweetly down her throat. When she had finished, she leaned over the edge of the bed and set down the tray. Then she decided that she might as well carry it out to the kitchen herself. It was ridiculous to have Alain waiting on her when she was perfectly fit herself. Swinging her legs over the side of the bed, she stood up and bent over to lift the tray. But she was unprepared for the sudden ringing in her ears and the way the floor seemed to rush up to meet her. The tray dropped from her fingers with a crash and she sat hastily down on the bed, burying her head in her lap and wondering why the room seemed to be whirling around her. She hardly heard the door burst open.

'What the hell are you doing now?' roared Alain from a great distance.

'Don't shout at me!' she wailed, lifting her head.

Then she burst into tears.

'Don't, Claire!' he begged, seizing her by the legs and bundling her back into bed. 'Don't. Don't cry, my love, please.'

She was dimly aware that he was holding her against him, stroking her tumbled hair and murmuring words of endearment to her. And aware too of something else. The room steadied around her and her sobs faded to a series of shuddering gulps. Drying her eyes on the sheet, she stared at him miserably.

'Don't call me that,' she begged.

'Call you what?' he asked in perplexity.

'"My love",' she said unsteadily.

'Why not?' he murmured. 'You are, you know.'

Her eyes filled with tears again and she had to bite on her lower lip to still its trembling. 'That's not true,' she choked. 'You hate me. You always have done.'

Alain's fingers gripped her damp hair, pinning it behind her ears. Gazing intently into her eyes, he shook his head.

'Wrong, Claire,' he replied. 'I've loved you from the first moment I saw you.'

CHAPTER EIGHT

'W-WHAT do you mean?' she faltered.

His eyes took on a distant look and a faint smile twisted the edges of his mouth.

'Six years ago I walked into a very modest little restaurant at Acajou Beach,' he murmured in the tone of someone thinking aloud. 'The smells from the kitchen were good and the proprietor was a big burly Tahitian called Roland Beaumont. He offered me a drink as casually as if I were a friend calling at his home and then he said he'd get his daughter to bring me a menu. You were outside waiting at the tables on the terrace and he shouted to you to come in. Do you remember? I looked up and there you were, standing in the doorway and laughing. The blue water of the lagoon was behind you and you were wearing a red pareu and flowers in your hair. I thought you were the most beautiful girl I'd ever seen in my life. I think I fell in love with you right then.'

Claire stared at him in disbelief. His words shocked her to the core and she suddenly found the events of the last six years hurtling through her mind like a blurred video as she tried to grasp the significance of what he was saying. But it was too unexpected, too unsettling. Her first instinctive joy gave way to a wary impulse to avoid being hurt.

'You're joking,' she said uncertainly.

Alain's grip on her hair tightened for an instant. Then suddenly he released her and clasped his hands moodily round his knee instead.

'No, I'm not joking,' he growled. 'I wish to God I were. But surely you must have guessed, Claire? Why did you think I came to your father's restaurant every day for lunch?'

'I don't know,' replied Claire blankly. 'I thought you liked the pancakes, I suppose.'

Alain's lips twisted into a crooked smile.

'And you never once guessed that you were the central attraction?' he demanded caustically. 'You never once thought of me as a man instead of just a customer?'

'Not exactly,' admitted Claire. 'You seemed so much older, so stern and forbidding somehow. Almost as if you belonged to a different generation.'

'I was twenty-seven,' said Alain with grim humour. 'I suppose to a nineteen-year-old that seems totally senile.'

A mischievous smile played around her lips as she saw Alain's discomfiture.

'I'll tell you something though,' she conceded. 'Even though you were so stern and forbidding, I had a dreadful crush on you. As a matter of fact, I practically worshipped the ground you walked on.'

Alain snorted.

'There's no need for you to invent these comforting little fantasies to soothe my pride,' he said drily.

'It's true!' insisted Claire. 'Anyway, if you were keen on me too, why didn't you invite me out? It would have made things so much simpler.'

A brooding look crossed Alain's face.

'Oddly enough,' he ground out, 'I didn't want to take advantage of your youth and innocence. Of course, Marcel had no such scruples.'

Claire flinched at the mention of that name.

'Don't,' she begged, her eyes clouding. 'Please don't. I can't bear it.'

'You can't bear it?' growled Alain. 'How the hell do you think I felt when I found out what you were doing? I could have murdered the man and you're damned lucky I didn't. Believe me, punching him in the nose and bullying you into leaving Tahiti was mild in comparison to what I wanted to do. I was so much on fire with jealousy I felt like going berserk.'

He very nearly had, Claire remembered. She thought of Marcel, groping his way out of the house with one hand clutched to his bleeding nose, of Alain shouting at her while she sobbed incoherently and wrapped her red pareu around her with shaking fingers.

'Is that why you were so hateful to me?' she asked unsteadily. 'Because you were jealous?'

He rose to his feet and paced moodily across the room, with his hands thrust deep into his pockets.

'Yes,' he said over his shoulder. 'Oh, I tried to pretend to myself that it was righteous fury on my sister's behalf, but the truth is that Louise hardly came into it. I would have felt like that about any man I found you in bed with. Hurt, betrayed, angry. Ridiculous, isn't it? Especially when you consider that I had never even told you how I felt about you. I thought that would be the end of it then. And yet, even once you had left, I never could stop loving you.'

'Never?' echoed Claire shakily.

Alain swung round.

'No!' he shouted. 'Damn it, that's what this is all about, isn't it? The fact that I'm as much in love with you as I ever was, no matter how badly you've treated me.'

'No matter how badly I've treated you?' spluttered Claire. 'You've got a nerve, Alain Charpentier! After you went off to Bora Bora for a passionate romp with your precious Nadine!'

'You really believe that, do you?' demanded Alain.

'What else can I believe?' retorted Claire with spirit. 'You were busy planning it the minute you hopped out of bed with me. I heard you discussing it with Nadine right in this very house, so don't bother denying it!'

Alain sighed.

'My only intention was for Nadine to come to Bora Bora with me to do some preliminary sketches for a new hotel,' he said in injured tones. 'Going to bed with her was not meant to be part of the package.'

'Really?' taunted Claire. 'But you still did it, didn't you?'

There was a moment's silence, fraught with tension. Even in that instant with her heart thudding unevenly and her nails dug into her palms, Claire was conscious of an overwhelming desire to hear Alain deny it. Her brown eyes met his in mute appeal and she saw a muscle twitch at his temple. He opened his mouth.

'Well, what do you think?' he challenged.

She could not believe the pain that throbbed through her at these words. A raw, scalding torment that made her catch her breath and wrap her arms protectively around her body.

'I hate you,' she whispered and buried her face in her huddled knees.

Alain crossed the floor with halting steps.

'Anyone would think you really cared,' he said hoarsely, sitting beside her and laying his hand on her head.

She jerked away from his touch as if it had burnt her.

'Of course I care!' she spat at him. 'Why else do you think I told you that I loved you that day we made love?'

Alain was silent, drawing in deep, shuddering breaths.

'I didn't realise you meant it,' he muttered at last. 'And I couldn't bear to think that you were just saying it as meaningless babble. If you were going to tell me you loved me, I wanted it to be real. The kind of blazing,

indestructible need that I felt for you. Not merely the
sort of thing you'd say as a pleasantry to every man you
slept with.'

'What do you mean "Every man I slept with"?' demanded Claire indignantly. 'I don't just go around
having casual affairs, I'll have you know!'

Alain's eyebrows rose.

'Well, there's been that cameraman Danny just in the
short time since you've been home,' he said.

'I didn't sleep with Danny!' protested Claire.

'Didn't you?' countered Alain bitterly. 'Well, that may
be true, although I have my doubts. And you certainly
went out of your way to make me believe it.'

'I only did that because I was jealous of you and
Nadine!' muttered Claire.

Alain ran his fingers through his hair with a baffled
sigh.

'Maybe,' he said sceptically. 'But you can't tell me
you don't have plenty of opportunities for torrid affairs
in the television industry.'

'Opportunities, yes. Involvements, no! After what
happened to me with Marcel, I've a damned good idea
of the amount of pain a reckless affair can let loose and
I've never fancied being burnt again.'

Alain stared at her in astonishment.

'Do you mean to tell me you've never slept with
another man since you and Marcel had your little reunion
in Sydney five years ago?' he demanded.

'Reunion?' echoed Claire in horror. 'What are you
talking about?'

'Oh, for heaven's sake!' snapped Alain. 'About a year
after you left here, Louise wrote to me from Sydney
saying Marcel was cheating on her and she was going to
file for a divorce. Naturally I assumed you were the girl
in question.'

'Well, I wasn't!' cried Claire hotly. 'I haven't seen Marcel since the day I left Tahiti and I hope I never do. If I learnt one thing from him, it was to be very, very wary about ever falling in love again. Not that that helped me much when it came to you.'

'Are you telling me that you were genuinely in love with me?' asked Alain slowly.

'I was,' replied Claire resentfully. 'Until you wrecked everything by going off with Nadine.'

A choking sob escaped her and she snatched the corner of the sheet and buried her face in it.

'Oh, Claire,' said Alain, sweeping her into his arms. 'I can see I'll have to tell you the truth about that. I didn't really intend to, but it seems cruel to go on deceiving you. The fact is that I didn't sleep with Nadine on Bora Bora.'

Claire's mouth fell open.

'But Marie Rose went there to check!' she protested indignantly. 'She saw the unit you were staying in and there was only one bed.'

Alain's lips curved in sardonic amusement.

'I had a feeling Marie Rose was there as your spy,' he murmured. 'And she saw exactly what I wanted her to see. Don't forget, Claire, that you had just sent me off to Bora Bora with the glad tidings that you were planning to sleep with Danny Abbott. Can you blame me for wanting to hit back? Once I knew that Marie Rose was coming to Bora Bora, I deliberately set things up to make her believe I was sleeping with Nadine. But it was sheer farce. The truth is that I was sleeping on the fold-out sofabed in the living-room.'

'Truly?' asked Claire suspiciously.

'Truly,' insisted Alain. His mouth was hard and his blue eyes were narrowed in a way that was almost resentful. 'Once I'd made love to you, I found that it seemed like sacrilege to think of touching another woman, however willing she might be.'

Claire gave him a swift, tormented look.

'Th-then Nadine was willing?' she whispered.

Alain's lips twisted into a smile that was closer to a sneer.

'Oh, yes. Willing to jump into bed with me, willing to let Marie Rose believe that I was her lover, willing even to marry me. But I wasn't tempted, Claire.'

'Why not?' croaked Claire. 'She's very attractive.'

'Because I don't love her, Claire, and she doesn't love me,' he replied simply. 'And, when I finally got over my rage and my hurt pride about you and Danny, I told Nadine the only sensible thing I could possibly say to her.'

'What do you mean?' she asked.

'I said that I was coming back from Bora Bora today so that I could ask you to marry me.'

'What?'

She was so shocked that she stared at him with her mouth open. Her heart accelerated wildly.

'You don't really mean that?' she said with an upward, questioning intonation.

'Oh, yes, I do!' vowed Alain. 'Look, Claire, I don't care any more what happened between you and Marcel or you and Danny. None of it matters. The only thing that matters is——'

'Alain, Danny and I didn't——' began Claire, but he brushed her protest aside and hauled her ruthlessly into his arms.

His lips met hers in a kiss that sent electric currents jolting through her veins. Then he looked down at her with intent blue eyes and let his fingers stray idly down her throat, playing with her tumbled dark hair.

'The only thing that matters is this,' he said fiercely. 'I want to wed you and bed you and spend the rest of my life with you. I love you more than any woman I've ever known. Will you marry me, Claire?'

For a moment she struggled to explain, to convince him, then she faltered to a stop as the meaning of his words sank in. Alain wanted to marry her. So did it even matter what he believed about Danny or Marcel?

She looked at him with misty eyes, then, threading her fingers through his springy dark hair, she drew his head down and kissed him.

'Yes,' she said. 'Oh, yes, my love.'

'We'll need to buy a ring,' said Alain the following morning as they were eating breakfast. 'What sort would you like?'

Claire stopped gazing dreamily out over the turquoise lagoon and brought her attention back to Alain. Her cheeks coloured and she smiled.

'Anything,' she replied fervently. 'A piece of string will do. So long as I'm marrying you, that's all that counts.'

Alain dropped a feather-light kiss on the back of her hand and then turned it over so that he could repeat it on her palm.

'My sentiments exactly,' he replied. 'You know, when we were in the church at Paul's and Marie's wedding, I couldn't help wondering if it would ever be us.'

'Did you?' marvelled Claire. 'So did I! Except I didn't really believe that it would. And when I caught Marie Rose's bouquet and you were so hateful to me I was certain of it. I thought I'd just be nobody's bride.'

Alain's eyes were shadowed with remorse. He gripped her hand so hard that it hurt.

'Well, all that anger and suspicion is in the past,' he assured her. 'And I'm sorry if I hurt you, Claire. But let's put it behind us and start spreading the good news. Now, who do we have to tell?'

'My parents,' replied Claire swiftly. 'They'll be thrilled. And Marie Rose and Paul. And your mother, I suppose.'

'And Louise,' said Alain.

Claire felt a chill of dismay settle in her stomach.

'Oh, Alain,' she faltered. 'I'd forgotten all about Louise. And it makes the whole thing impossible! How can she ever want to meet me when she knows I once had an affair with her husband?'

Alain frowned at her.

'Don't be absurd,' he said curtly, reaching for the coffee-pot. 'Louise doesn't know about you and Marcel. Why would she? She was in Paris when it happened.'

Claire blinked, still feeling shocked, but no longer in the grip of that icy dismay.

'B-but I thought you must have told her!' she stammered.

'Told her?' echoed Alain incredulously. 'Don't be ridiculous, Claire! My only concern at the time was to hush it all up to avoid hurting Louise and damaging your reputation.'

A wave of relief washed through Claire's entire body, but her fears would not be totally calmed.

'Then why didn't she come to Paul's and Marie Rose's wedding if she wasn't trying to avoid me?' she asked unhappily.

Alain smiled.

'Well, I had no idea at the time,' he replied. 'But I know now, because she's written and told me. Louise is expecting her first baby and she was laid low by morning sickness. That's all, Claire, I promise you. So you needn't have any fears about meeting her. Your relationship with Marcel is safely buried in the past and that's where it's going to stay!'

And with that Claire had to be content. Yet, all the same, she could not suppress a lurking sense of misgiving. Would the ripples from the past ever really stop spreading?

The rest of the week flew by. Alain, with his usual demonic energy, was busy with a dozen different things at once. The Heiva I Tahiti, the annual July festival, was in full swing and he was involved in organising many of the events. Yet he still found time to have the Beaumonts' wrecked car towed away and replaced, to send a plumber to mend their hot water service and remove their old bath and to take Claire out to choose an engagement ring. They went to the finest jeweller in town and Alain insisted on buying Claire not only a diamond ring, but also a magnificent black pearl necklace and matching earrings.

'Are you sure you like them?' he asked as she stood, pirouetting in front of a mirror in the shop. 'I want you to have whatever you like now, and don't worry about the cost.'

'They're beautiful,' breathed Claire, raising her left hand to her ears to touch the lustrous, silvery balls. The light winked off her ring finger as she did so. 'And so is the ring.'

Flinging herself into his arms, she gave a little shiver.

'What is it?' he asked.

'It all seems so much more real when I see the ring on my finger. It's rather scary.'

'You're not getting cold feet, are you?' he asked abruptly.

She shook her head, clutching at his arms.

'No,' she insisted. 'It's only scary because I can't believe I can possibly be so happy. I keep feeling afraid that something will go wrong.'

Alain snorted contemptuously.

'Well, if anything is going to go wrong,' he pointed out, 'it had better happen soon. There isn't much time left.'

That was true. Neither of them had seen any reason to delay their wedding. The engagement was to be publicly announced at the gala ball on the evening before Bastille Day and they were to be married a month later. Claire had already moved into Alain's house, an action which her parents regarded with easygoing tolerance, and she was already deep in planning her wedding dress and her honeymoon. As Alain said, if anything was going to go wrong, it had better happen soon.

On the night of the ball, Claire felt as if she had never been happier in her life. Dressed in a stunning evening frock of red silk taffeta, she clung to Alain's arm and smiled radiantly as the mayor announced their engagement. A noisy outburst of cheering followed and, during the remainder of the evening, all Alain's friends and business acquaintances thronged to congratulate them. All but one. As they were leaving the ball shortly after two a.m., Claire felt a cold, hard grip on her arm. She turned and saw Nadine Hugo staring at her with venomous golden eyes.

'I suppose you think you've done very well for yourself, don't you?' the French girl hissed. 'Well, let me tell you, Claire Beaumont, you're going to regret the day you ever became engaged to Alain Charpentier!'

That was all. But something in the tone of Nadine's voice made Claire's blood curdle. She twisted frantically in Nadine's hard, pinching grip, looking for Alain over the heads of the crowd. Then suddenly she caught sight of him.

'Alain!' she exclaimed.

In the milling crowd he had already become separated from her and was standing with his head bent chatting to someone. But at the sound of Claire's voice, his glossy, dark head came up and his blue eyes narrowed.

'Is something wrong?' he asked.

With a final determined effort, Claire pulled free of Nadine's grip. She didn't want to make a scene in such a public place, but she couldn't wait to escape. Turning her back on Nadine, she elbowed her way towards Alain and took his arm. At once she felt safe again and was even able to give him a rather strained smile.

'No, nothing's wrong,' she mumbled. 'But I am rather tired. Couldn't we go now?'

They had to edge past Nadine again to make their way out to the car park. Alain spoke civilly to her and she stood on tiptoe to kiss him on both cheeks. Then, to Claire's horror, she did the same thing to her.

'Remember what I told you, Claire, won't you?' she murmured sweetly, as she retreated into the crowd.

Claire shuddered.

'What the hell did she tell you?' demanded Alain once they were in the car.

'She . . . she said I'd regret the day I ever became engaged to you,' replied Claire unhappily.

Alain snorted with laughter.

'Is that all?' he demanded. 'I thought she'd sent you a death threat at the very least, you were looking so upset. But you shouldn't take any notice of Nadine. Once she gets over her hurt pride, she'll realise that it would have been a total disaster for both of us if I'd married her. Anyway, she certainly won't do anything to hurt you.'

'I hope you're right,' said Claire doubtfully.

Alain reached out and squeezed her hand.

'Stop worrying, sweetheart,' he ordered. 'Or if you must worry about something, worry about whether your dance troupe is going to win a prize in the *tamure* competition this week.'

'All right,' promised Claire with a glimmer of a smile.

Astonishingly they did win the *tamure* competition and were invited to perform at a winners' concert the following Saturday. Claire knew that she should have been walking on air. She was engaged to a man she loved with all her heart, her father was making a good recovery from his illness and she was back on the island that she loved. Yet all week she felt an uneasy sense of disaster hanging over her like the threat of a storm. She could not help brooding over the veiled menace contained in Nadine's words and her anxiety showed itself in an unaccustomed listlessness and loss of spirits.

'Are you sure you aren't having second thoughts about marrying me?' Alain demanded as she was dressing in her costume on the night of the concert.

'Of course not!' retorted Claire in dismay, pausing as she adjusted her head garland in front of the mirrored dressing-table. 'Whatever gave you that idea?'

'You've seemed so gloomy all week. I wish you'd promise me that you really are happy and you really will marry me.'

Claire's lips curved into a joyful smile. Leaning forward, she took his face in hers and stared intently at him, as if she were memorising every detail of his features. The sardonic eyebrows, the smouldering blue eyes, the mobile, rather arrogant mouth.

'I promise,' she said huskily. And kissed him.

As always, the potent flame of sexual longing flared between them and she heard his strangled groan as her mouth opened sweetly against his. Rising to his feet, he stood staring down at her with an expression that sent tingles of excitement chasing through her entire body.

'Don't think I'm not tempted,' he muttered. 'But you've got this wretched concert down on the waterfront in an hour's time and I have to see the banquet manager at the hotel before I leave. I think for once we'll have to postpone our passion, don't you?'

Claire ran her hand shamelessly down over the front of his shorts and moved her fingers in a caressing circle.

'Yes,' she murmured softly.

Alain caught his breath.

'Sometimes,' he muttered through his teeth. 'I'm not sure whether I ought to strangle you or——'

'Or?' prompted Claire wickedly.

'You'll find out soon enough, wench,' he growled. 'In the meantime, finish getting dressed. I'll go over and speak to the banquet manager. I should be back in ten minutes, so be ready. OK?'

Claire pushed away her vague feelings of disquiet and hummed softly to herself as she put the finishing touches to her costume of grass skirt, beaded top, shell necklace and floral head garland. There was no doubt about it. All she would have to do tonight was think about Alain and she would dance the erotic *tamure* with more sizzling intensity than ever before. Fanning her long, dark hair in a loose, swirling curtain around her shoulders, she curved her lips and applied some red lipstick. Just at that moment, the front door bell rang. With a puzzled frown, Claire dropped the lipstick and went to answer it. Perhaps Alain had forgotten his key.

But it was not Alain who stood there on the front veranda. It was a man Claire had never expected to see again. She staggered back in disbelief as her stunned brain took in the details of the tall, swaggering figure, the brown hair brushed back from the forehead, the melting brown eyes and the calculated charm of that gleaming smile.

'M-Marcel Sauvage!' she croaked.

He took advantage of her shock to open the door and stride into the hall, with the air of a cowboy challenging a saloon full of spectators.

'Just a minute!' protested Claire hotly. 'Who asked you to——?'

'Oh, come on, sweetheart,' crooned Marcel in that husky, theatrical voice that she had once thought un-

believably sexy. 'I've got a business proposition to put
to you.'

Claire was still staring at him in disbelief. Now that
she looked more closely, she saw that he had aged a lot
in the past six years. His jawline was blurred with fat
and there were broken purple veins in his nose and
cheeks. Within another five years he would look like an
old man.

'Business proposition?' she echoed with a half hys-
terical laugh. 'Don't be a fool, Marcel! I've no intention
of doing business with you now or ever. Anyway how
did you know I was here?'

He smiled slyly.

'Nadine told me,' he said. 'We're old friends, you
know, from our long association with the Charpentiers.
And she thought you'd be just the girl I need as
anchorwoman for a new TV series I'm doing in France.
I'll pay top dollar to get you, *chérie*. You've come on a
lot from the gawky little teenager I first knew a few years
ago. And who knows? We might even be able to mix
pleasure with business. I'm sure you'd find a part-
nership with me far more rewarding than throwing
yourself away on that pillar of society, Alain
Charpentier.'

The venom in his tone as he spoke Alain's name was
unmistakable. Claire felt a surge of molten rage flood
through her veins at his impertinence. When she replied,
her voice was shaking with anger.

'Don't you dare speak to me about Alain,' she cried.
'Or about your slimy business propositions. I don't want
to see you again, Marcel, now or ever.'

Marcel chuckled hoarsely.

'Still playing hard to get?' he demanded. 'Well, I know
how to deal with that, don't I, sweetheart?'

And before Claire could do anything more than utter a stifled shriek of outrage, he seized her in his arms, let her dangle backwards and kissed her violently.

'Mmpph! You bastard...you absolute...mmmpph! Let me go...I'll kill you!'

She struck out wildly, trying to scratch his face or knee him in the groin. But because of the ridiculous position that he held her in, the only result was that when she raised one foot, she lost her balance completely. With a muffled scream she fell to the floor, taking Marcel with her. His full weight slammed into her and for a moment she lay dazed, unable to do anything but choke for breath. Marcel's hands scrabbled eagerly at her beaded top and his ravenous kisses covered her throat.

'Oh, you're some passionate baby,' he cried. 'You drive me wild, sweetheart. And I knew you'd be just as pleased to see me as I am to see you. This ice-maiden act doesn't fool me for a minute.'

But before he could go any further, there was the sound of the front door being flung wide and a sudden, startled oath. Marcel was torn off her and shaken like a rat. She sat up unsteadily to see his shirt being twisted into a convenient handle before he was hurled bodily out into the garden. Letting out a long, unsteady sigh, she levered herself to her feet.

'Oh, Alain,' she gasped. 'Thank heavens you came!'

There was no answering smile on his face. Instead, he looked as if he was in a killing rage. Only once in her life had Claire ever seen him so furious before and now she had the nightmare sensation of that appalling scene being played out a second time over. Alain's blue eyes were like narrow slits in a face dark with anger and his mouth was set in a grim line.

'What exactly were you doing with Marcel?' he asked with menacing softness.

Claire shook her head in disbelief.

'You surely don't think——?' she began.

'What else am I supposed to think?' he demanded furiously. 'I came home to find you half naked rolling around on the floor with Marcel. Am I supposed to think you were offering him a cup of coffee?'

'How dare you?' cried Claire shakily.

Coming hot on the heels of her ordeal with Marcel, this was more than she could bear. With an angry sob, she raised her hand and slapped Alain's face with all her force. His head jerked back and four red marks leapt out on his cheek. He advanced on her with icy fury and at that moment there was the sound of delicate throat-clearing from the veranda.

'Sorry,' called Nadine's voice sweetly. 'I do seem to have come at rather a bad time, don't I?'

Claire stared in horror at the chic figure on the doorstep. Every ginger hair was neatly in place, the lips were painted in a perfect Cupid's bow and there was an unmistakable gloating look in Nadine's eyes as if she had planned every detail of Claire's humiliation. With a jolt of horror, Claire realised that she had.

'Oh, go away!' she choked. And slammed the door in Nadine's face.

Which left her alone with Alain.

'What? You don't want Nadine to see you behaving like a street walker?' asked Alain sarcastically.

Claire clenched her fists.

'Oh, don't be so stupid!' she cried. 'She must have set the whole thing up! Surely you can see that?'

'Nadine?' retorted Alain incredulously. 'Nadine set it up?'

'Yes!'

'How?'

'I don't know all the details!' cried Claire angrily, straightening her beaded bodice, which was slipping off her breasts. 'But Marcel said she told him I was here and suggested he offer me a job in France. If I had accepted, it would have cleared the way for her. When I didn't, Marcel obviously jumped at the chance to humiliate me. And you.'

'Don't be ridiculous!' snapped Alain.

'I'm not being half as ridiculous as you are!' retorted Claire. 'Surely you don't honestly believe I was encouraging him?'

'I don't know what I believe!' said Alain bitterly. 'But I know what I saw and it's every bit as bad as what I saw six years ago.'

'Six years ago!' exclaimed Claire. 'That's the whole trouble between us, isn't it, Alain? The fact that you can never wipe out what you saw six years ago! And, if I marry you, you'll let it spoil every minute of our future together. You know, Marie Rose told me that we had a big problem with trust and she was right. Well, I learnt to trust you, Alain, but you've never really learnt to trust me, have you? And that's just not good enough for me. So, unless you apologise to me right now for your ridiculous, unfounded suspicions, I'm leaving!'

She stared at him with blazing eyes and quivering lips, fully expecting that he would sweep her into his arms and beg her forgiveness. But his face remained like an angry, suspicious mask and the silence lengthened agonisingly between them.

'All right, then!' said Claire hoarsely, twisting the diamond ring off her finger and setting it on the table. 'If that's the way you want it, goodbye, Alain, and good luck.'

Clenching her fist, she pressed it against her lips and ran into the bedroom. Out of habit she still kept her passport and traveller's cheques in her purse and it wouldn't be difficult to catch a plane out of Papeete. She had thought her gypsy lifestyle was finished forever, but obviously she had been wrong. It took her less than

a minute to stuff a change of clothes into an overnight
bag and she was ready to go. Dashing away the tears,
she went back into the hall with the bag in her hand.
Amazingly her voice came out clear and steady.

'In the circumstances, I'm sure you'll want me to leave
as fast as possible,' she said coldly. 'But there's no need
for you to drive me this time. I'll borrow your second
car and leave it in the airport car park, unless you've
some objection?'

He didn't answer. He was standing with his head
bowed and one hand covering his eyes. As she came
closer to the hall table, she saw that his face looked drawn
and haggard with torment. But he made no move to stop
her as she went past him.

'Goodbye, Alain,' she repeated.

She was almost into Papeete when the first real shock
hit her. Her hands began to tremble on the steering-wheel
and she had to pull over to the kerb for fear of having
an accident. As she did so, she glanced unthinkingly at
her watch. It was seven forty-five p.m.

'Oh, hell, the concert!' she groaned.

The last thing she wanted to do at this moment was
to dance the *tamure* before hundreds of spectators, but
she couldn't bear the thought of letting down her friends.
Everyone would be waiting for her and if she really
stepped on the accelerator she could still make it on time.

It was two minutes to eight when she jumped out of
the car on the waterfront at the Boulevard Pomare and
sprinted through the crowd to the performers' entrance
at the festival grandstand. An excited chorus greeted her.

'Where have you been, Claire?'

'We phoned and phoned Alain's house, but there was
no answer.'

'What happened to your head garland? It's ripped
to shreds!'

'We were going to send Matilde on to dance, but she's not half as good as you.'

'Shush, girls! We're on next.'

Somewhere a fresh head garland was found for Claire and a moment later she found herself thrust out into the floodlit square with the tiers of darkened seats around her. Into the tense waiting silence came the low, insistent throbbing of the drums and suddenly Claire forgot all about Alain and surrendered totally to the rhythm of the dance. And yet somehow all her love and grief and anger flowed into her movements, so that when the troupe finally stamped to a halt, there was a wild outburst of cheers and whistles. Claire smiled and bowed with the others, but there was an ache in her heart as she made her way offstage. Dazzled by the floodlights, she did not even see the shadowy figure near the dressing-room door until a hand came out of the darkness and touched her. She let out a stifled shriek.

'It's all right, Claire. It's only me.'

'Alain,' she breathed. Then recovered her poise and hastily added, 'Leave me alone.'

'I need to talk to you,' he insisted.

'There's nothing more to be said,' she snapped.

'Yes, there is,' he protested, hauling her into the centre of the passage where there was more light. 'There's everything to be said. Just give me five minutes, Claire. That's all I ask.'

People were streaming around them and someone stepped on Claire's toe.

'Ouch!' she said.

'Five minutes,' repeated Alain. 'You might as well come, Claire, because I'll carry you if I have to.'

She cast him a smouldering look.

'I'm not impressed by caveman tactics,' she muttered resentfully.

Yet when he took her arm, she allowed him to lead
her out on to the docks. The air was warm and mild and
the ships in the harbour were strung with lights, which
sent golden reflections dancing over the water. An en-
ticing medley of scents wafted from the take-away food
vans further along the waterfront and in the distance she
could hear the sound of hurdy-gurdy music from a fair-
ground. But here, behind the dance area, it was surprisingly quiet and private. Alain led Claire across to the
water's edge.

'Well?' she demanded sharply.

His hand on her arm was sending unwelcome surges
of emotion coursing through her and she was afraid that
at any moment she might burst into tears.

'I've come to say I'm sorry,' he said.

Claire hunched her shoulder away from his touch.

'Oh?' she sneered. 'Won't Nadine object to that?'

'Never mind Nadine!' exclaimed Alain. 'I've decided
you were right about her and I've paid her not to do the
blueprints for the new hotel. With luck we'll never set
eyes on her again.'

Claire stared at him in astonishment.

'What brought this on?' she asked suspiciously.

'I'll tell you!' he replied, gripping her shoulders and
forcing her to look at him. 'After you'd left, I sat down
and took a good look at myself and I didn't much like
what I saw.'

'What do you mean?' demanded Claire.

'Do I have to spell it out?' growled Alain. 'All right,
then. I will. There's no way you could have been re-
sponsible for what happened tonight and I should never
have accused you of it. I was arrogant, I was stupid, I
was wrong!'

'Yes, you were,' agreed Claire fervently. 'So why
couldn't you see all that immediately? Why did it take
you this long to figure it out?'

Alain raked his fingers through his hair and let out an impatient sigh.

'Try to understand, Claire!' he urged. 'When I walked in there tonight, it was like a flashback to the past. I was so shocked and furious to see Marcel that I didn't react with my brain, I reacted with my hormones. And it took me a while to simmer down enough to realise that you were completely innocent. Can you forgive me, Claire?'

Claire's mouth set in a mulish line.

'Even if I do,' she said in a shaking voice, 'what's going to happen next time there's any situation that's remotely compromising? Are you going to fly into a rage because you see me smiling at a bell boy or kissing a friend on the cheek?'

Alain swore under his breath.

'No!' he insisted.

'How can I be sure of that?' demanded Claire.

Alain took her hands in his and kissed them urgently.

'You can be sure of it because I finally have come to terms with the past,' he said. 'And I'll never misjudge you again. After you left tonight, I realised that I was being stupid, because I started to think of all the things I knew about you. I knew you gave up your own career to help out your family in times of trouble. I knew you were loyal and kind and that everybody liked you. And I realised that you were totally incapable of doing anything heartless or deceitful. I don't believe that you knew Marcel was married or that you slept with Danny. Whatever you choose to do now, I had to find you and tell you that.'

Claire's lips quirked into a reluctant smile.

'How did you find me?' she asked.

Alain's hands cupped her face and he stroked her cheeks with his thumbs. He smiled ruefully.

'I also knew you'd never let your friends down when they were counting on you,' he murmured. 'Oh, Claire. I'd trust you with my honour, my love, my life. I only wish you'd do the same with me.'

His lips touched her hair, moved down to meet hers. Arching her back, she put her arms around his neck and let her body rest trustingly against his.

'All right,' she said, relenting. 'I will.'

ESCAPE INTO ANOTHER WORLD...

...With Temptation Dreamscape Romances

Two worlds collide in 3 very special Temptation titles, guaranteed to sweep you to the very edge of reality.

The timeless mysteries of reincarnation, telepathy and earthbound spirits clash with the modern lives and passions of ordinary men and women.

Available November 1993   Price £5.55

MILLS & BOON

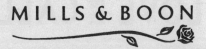

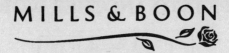

Accept 4 FREE Romances and 2 FREE gifts

FROM READER SERVICE

Here's an irresistible invitation from Mills & Boon. Please accept our offer of 4 FREE Romances, a CUDDLY TEDDY and a special MYSTERY GIFT! Then, if you choose, go on to enjoy 6 captivating Romances every month for just £1.80 each, postage and packing FREE. Plus our FREE Newsletter with author news, competitions and much more.

Send the coupon below to: Mills & Boon Reader Service, FREEPOST, PO Box 236, Croydon, Surrey CR9 9EL.

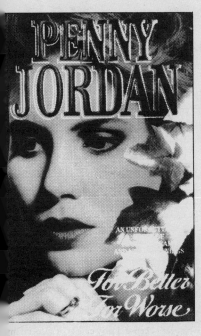

Next Month's Romances

Each month you can choose from a wide variety of romance with Mills & Boon. Below are the new titles to look out for next month, why not ask either Mills & Boon Reader Service or your Newsagent to reserve you a copy of the titles you want to buy – just tick the titles you would like and either post to Reader Service or take it to any Newsagent and ask them to order your books.

Please save me the following titles:	Please tick	✓
DAWN SONG	Sara Craven	
FALLING IN LOVE	Charlotte Lamb	
MISTRESS OF DECEPTION	Miranda Lee	
POWERFUL STRANGER	Patricia Wilson	
SAVAGE DESTINY	Amanda Browning	
WEST OF BOHEMIA	Jessica Steele	
A HEARTLESS MARRIAGE	Helen Brooks	
ROSES IN THE NIGHT	Kay Gregory	
LADY BE MINE	Catherine Spencer	
SICILIAN SPRING	Sally Wentworth	
A SCANDALOUS AFFAIR	Stephanie Howard	
FLIGHT OF FANTASY	Valerie Parv	
RISK TO LOVE	Lynn Jacobs	
DARK DECEIVER	Alex Ryder	
SONG OF THE LORELEI	Lucy Gordon	
A TASTE OF HEAVEN	Carol Grace	

If you would like to order these books in addition to your regular subscription from Mills & Boon Reader Service please send £1.80 per title to: Mills & Boon Reader Service, Freepost, P.O. Box 236, Croydon, Surrey, CR9 9EL, quote your Subscriber No:.................................. (If applicable) and complete the name and address details below. Alternatively, these books are available from many local Newsagents including W.H.Smith, J.Menzies, Martins and other paperback stockists from 3 December 1993.

Name:...

Address:...

....Post Code:..........................

To Retailer: If you would like to stock M&B books please contact your regular book/magazine wholesaler for details.

You may be mailed with offers from other reputable companies as a result of this application.
If you would rather not take advantage of these opportunities please tick box ☐